The Perfect Place

The Perfect Place

by

Teresa E. Harris

CLARION BOOKS

Houghton Mifflin Harcourt

Boston   New York

Clarion Books

215 Park Avenue South, New York, New York 10003

Copyright © 2014 by Teresa E. Harris

All rights reserved. For information about permission to reproduce selections from this book, write to trade.permissions@hmhco.com or to Permissions, Houghton Mifflin Harcourt Publishing Company, 3 Park Avenue, 19th Floor, New York, New York 10016.

Clarion Books is an imprint of Houghton Mifflin Harcourt Publishing Company.

www.hmhco.com

The text was set in Filosophia.

Library of Congress Cataloging-in-Publication Data
Harris, Teresa E.
The perfect place / Teresa E. Harris.
pages cm
Summary: Twelve-year-old Treasure Daniels and her younger sister must move in with Great-aunt Grace until their mother sorts herself out, but life in Black Lake, Virginia, where segregation lingers, is hard and Grace is a nightmare—at least on the surface.
ISBN 978-1-328-77394-4 (paperback)
[1. Home—Fiction. 2. Family life—Virginia—Fiction. 3. Great-aunts—Fiction. 4. Segregation—Fiction. 5. African Americans—Fiction. 6. Moving, Household—Fiction. 7. Virginia—Fiction.] I. Title.
PZ7.H24388Per 2014
[Fic]—dc23
2013036214

Manufactured in the United States of America
DOC 10 9 8 7 6 5 4 3 2 1

4500639308

For Taana

One

DAD has been gone exactly two months, one week, and four days when Mom stands up and says, "I can't do this anymore."

"Do what?" I ask.

"This," she says, waving her skinny brown arms around like a crazy person. "Stay here in this apartment. I can't do it. Your father is everywhere in it."

"No, he's not," my sister Tiffany says, looking around from her spot beside me on the couch. She's seven and what my sixth-grade teacher, Mrs. Levy, would have called very literal-minded.

But Mom is right, I guess. Dad is everywhere in Apartment 2F—his coffee mug is still in the dish drainer and all but two pairs of his shoes are still lined up against the far wall in Mom and Dad's bedroom. The book he's reading is still sitting on his nightstand. I like the way the house seems to be waiting along with us for him to come back. But Mom says it again: "I can't do this."

"What are we going to do, then?" I ask.

Mom doesn't answer. Instead she goes over to the framed pictures on the mantel. She slides the photo of the four of us at the Meadowlands Fair from one location to another like a game of magic-cup shuffle until it winds up at the far end of the shelf almost out of sight and right beside the picture of her steely-eyed aunt Grace. Mom stares down at Great-Aunt Grace's picture for a long time, and I wonder if she's thinking about how, on their wedding day, Great-Aunt Grace told Mom not to marry Dad because he was a rolling stone if she ever saw one. Mom told me this story once when she was mad at Dad for staying out for two days and neglecting to call. I asked Mom what it meant to be a rolling stone and she pressed her lips together and shook her head, like she was sorry she'd told me the story in the first place.

Mom turns to face us now.

Please don't say we have to leave without Dad.

Tiffany moves closer to me on the couch, rests all of her weight on me. I can't breathe. I take a puff of my inhaler. The cool air fills my lungs.

Don't say we have to leave without Dad.

"What are we going to do?" I ask again, my heart banging against my ribs like a paddleball.

"We're going to evacuate the premises," Mom says.

"We don't have to go," I say.

Tiffany stands beside me, hopping from one foot to the other as she waits for me to take her leftover brown rice and baked chicken out of the microwave. She has no idea what "evacuate the premises" means. Mom learned the trick from Dad—whenever he decided that it was time for us to move, he'd find a new, crazy-hard way to tell Mom and me so that Tiffany wouldn't understand and freak out.

I pull the cover off of Tiffany's plate. Steam hits me full in the face.

"You can eat in front of the TV," Mom tells her.

"No, she can't." Dad never allowed us to eat anywhere but at the dining room or kitchen table. This type of disagreement has been happening between Mom and me ever since he left. She usually wins because she plays the parent card and says, "I'm her mother, Treasure, not you." That's exactly what she says this time as she stands at the sink, staring out the window. Her voice is so quiet it could be carried away on the breeze ruffling the curtains.

Tiffany scampers off, and I look at Mom long and hard. Her feet are bare, her toenails unpainted. She's wearing a black tank top and black denim shorts. She's been wearing a lot of black lately. I wait until Tiffany turns on the TV and starts singing along with the *SpongeBob SquarePants* theme song before I start talking.

"What about your job?" I ask.

"What about it?" Mom replies. "I answer phones for Dr. Jackass, and I won't miss him or his stuck-up patients at all."

I take a seat at the kitchen table and stare at the back of my mother's head, the tight curls of her bun. I'm not giving up so easily.

"If we leave, Dad won't know where to find us when he comes back."

Mom uses both hands to push herself away from the kitchen counter. Then she comes over to the table and lowers herself into the chair across from me. She reaches for the half-empty pepper shaker and begins to push it back and forth over the scratched wood surface. "And whose fault is it that he won't be able to find us?"

My skin is a different shade from hers, reddish-brown like Dad's. I have his confused hair, too, hair that doesn't know if it wants to be curly, nappy, or straight. I don't look a thing like Mom. I could walk away from her in a crowd and no one would even know we were related.

"We can't leave," I say.

Mom wraps her long fingers around the pepper shaker and stares down at her fist.

"I won't leave. Are you listening to me, Mom? *Mom?*" I hate the way my voice sounds, high and whiny, and Mom isn't even paying attention. I bang my fist down on the table.

She jumps. "What the—?" She shakes her head.

"You're just a child, Treasure, and you don't make the decisions. I do."

Just a child who walked Tiffany to school every morning after Dad left. Who did the grocery shopping and made sure Tiffany had something to eat every day. Who took Mom food on a tray when she couldn't get out of bed.

"What if we found him?" I say suddenly.

All this time Mom hasn't been looking at me. Now she does. "How?" she says, and for a moment I can hear it in her voice—hope. I don't know how we can find Dad, though; wouldn't even know where to start.

Mom closes her eyes. "Wishful thinking," she says. And just like that, I know nothing I say is going to change her mind. We're going to evacuate the premises, leaving Dad behind.

Two

I am lying in bed, eyes closed, when Mom comes for us. I feel her standing in the doorway of our room. She comes inside, and I don't have to open my eyes to know that she is standing at the foot of my bed, a suitcase in her hand, two bags at her feet.

"We have to go."

"Now?" I ask.

The light from the streetlamp outside filters into the room, lifting the darkness just enough for me to see the outline of my mother. I watch as she goes over to Tiffany's bed and shakes her. Tiffany mumbles something and won't wake up. I stay where I am. It's not like we haven't moved before, but we've never done it in the middle of the night, and never without Dad.

"I'm not going," I say. "And neither is Tiffany."

"Fine," Mom whispers. "Then I hope you two have some money to give to Mr. Brown when he comes sniffing around for the rent."

I sit up so fast I get dizzy. "What do you mean? You haven't been paying the rent?"

"I paid what I could, but it still wasn't enough."

"How much do we owe?"

"I don't know, a thousand dollars, maybe more. Mr. Brown stopped by to yell at me about it the other day, talking about eviction and whatnot—"

"*Eviction?*" It dawns on me suddenly why we're leaving in the middle of the night, why Mom is dressed all in black, whispering and slipping in and out of the darkness like a shadow. "So we couldn't stay here even if we wanted to?"

"Nope. Not unless you or your sister have a gang of money in your piggy banks you never told me about."

I don't have a gang of money. Or a piggy bank. And all Tiffany has is her Disney Fund, a three-gallon water bottle where she keeps the change that she's saving up for a trip to Disney World. A few dollars, maybe.

I climb out of bed and start taking off my PJs.

Our building is only four floors, and as luck would have it, our second-floor apartment is right above Mr. Brown's. Mom switches on the lamp on the night table between our beds. Quick and quiet as a cat, she pulls clothes from dressers, toys from shelves. It is when she is pulling down Tiffany's dollhouse that something comes crashing down with it and hits the floor with a thud. A photo album.

We both freeze. And wait. Nothing.

Mom makes her way over to my desk, more careful this time, and tosses me my jean shorts and T-shirt from the back of my chair. I love that chair. Dad bought it for me. It's purple and it spins around and around.

I pull on my shorts and top and take my time with my socks, rolling them down my ankles into perfect doughnut shapes. When I stand up and tiptoe over to grab my sneakers, Mom rips the sheets and comforter off my bed. She folds them up fast and comes back for the pillows. She pulls off the cases and shoves as much of our clothes as she can into them. Within moments, Mom's got most of our stuff in a pile by the bedroom door. Except for my chair.

"What about . . . ?" I point.

"Not enough room. Let's go."

Dad would never make me leave my chair.

Mom focuses her attention on getting Tiffany up. When she finally succeeds, the first thing Tiffany does is start whimpering.

"No time for that," Mom tells her, yanking Tiffany's T-shirt over her head. She puts on the rest of Tiffany's clothes in the same rough manner. Then she pulls the sheets from Tiffany's bed, knocking Tiffany's ratty yellow bear, Mr. Teddy Daniels, to the floor in the process. I pick him up and hand him to Tiffany, who squeezes him to her chest.

"Come on," Mom says.

She tiptoes out of our bedroom and we follow. Tiffany trips over a lump in the carpet in the hallway. Mom pulls her up by her arm and Tiffany whines. No use, though. All Mom is seeing right now is the path from the apartment to the car. She keeps her finger to her lips.

When we reach the living room, she points straight ahead, meaning we're going right to the door. No detours.

"Treasure, where are you—"

Mom knows better than to raise her voice.

I stop at the bookshelves and grab Dad's favorite dictionary, the one he always pulled down to teach me new words. I know where it is, even with only the streetlights to guide me.

"Treasure," Mom whisper-yells. She says my name again when I come to stand next to her and Tiffany, only this time she sounds tired, not mad. "Let's go."

Mom had already been down to the car a few times before she woke us up, but there's still the stuff from our bedroom to be carried downstairs. Tiffany whines again because she wants to be carried too, but Mom tells her to cut it out, and none too nicely, either. Mom says this time down is the last trip—we have to get out of here before Mr. Brown catches us. I grab as much as I can.

"Tiffany, put that bear in here and carry this." Mom holds a bulging pillowcase open. Reluctantly, Tiffany places Mr. Teddy Daniels gently inside and takes the pillowcase. Mom makes Tiffany carry a few other things too, and Tiffany does so with limp arms and tears in her eyes.

We will take the back stairs, Mom tells us—someone might see us on the elevator—and hold our breath, praying we make not even one sound.

Mom pushes open the door to the stairs. The stairwell echoes like the inside of a tin can. First Tiffany and then me. Mom is last.

I know before my foot hits the first step that I should've stopped to put the dictionary in my backpack. Carrying it and trying to hold on to two dolls and a pillowcase full of clothes, my arms tremble and then burn. My muscles tell me to let go, and I do. Everything falls and hits the floor. The dictionary hits the hardest.

"Jesus Christ, Treasure," Mom yelps.

My heart is beating somewhere in my throat and I'm ready to cry. But there's no time for that. When I reach down to gather the things as fast as I can, Mom stops me with a finger to her lips.

"Shhh!"

What did she hear? If Mr. Brown finds us here, he'll have every right to call the cops. Tiffany looks up at me from a few stairs below, stricken.

We all listen now. Silence. Mom swears. She never does that unless she's fighting mad.

"Sorry," I whisper, as we pick up the things I've dropped.

Mom doesn't look at the stuff as she shoves what she can into my arms and takes the rest herself. But she doesn't get it all. There, just there, on the step right below me, is Dad's dictionary. I reach for it.

"Leave it."

Mom stares down at it. Her face is unreadable.

"Leave it," she says again.

I do. And feel something inside me break.

~~~~~~

Mom helps us dump the rest of our things in the back of our Ford Explorer. The truck gleams blue and silver in the moonlight. Dad bought it used for Mom three years ago as a surprise, and she hated it from the moment she laid eyes on it, I could tell. She'd never said so until after Dad left this time. Every day now she says something about how it's so ugly it practically makes her eyes bleed. In goes my nebulizer, which Tiffany dubbed my asthma machine, followed by the pillowcases full of clothes from our bedroom and Tiffany's Disney Fund.

"Wait! I want Mr. Teddy Daniels," Tiffany says, and Mom sucks her teeth because she forgot which pillowcase he was in. She finds him at last and thrusts him at Tiffany, who asks, "Did you remember to pack his clothes?"

"Yes," Mom replies, and goes back to packing the truck.

"Are you sure?"

Mom whirls around.

"She's sure, Tiffany," I say quickly to avoid a meltdown. "I saw her pack them myself."

Tiffany nods, satisfied. I didn't see Mom pack Mr.

Teddy D.'s clothes, but she probably did it before she woke us up. She'd never leave his stuff behind.

My eyes find the face of our apartment building. There's a plaque above the back door, and above it a dim, buzzing light. I know that the plaque reads APARTMENT'S FOR RENT. FOR MORE INFORMATION CALL BROWN & ASSOCIATES AT 973-627-3746. There was scarcely a time we went through the back door that Dad didn't stop and draw our attention to that plaque and what he called the "reckless apostrophe" in APARTMENT'S.

Mom finishes loading up the truck. She goes around the side and opens the back door, calling us over with a jerk of her head. We don't move.

"Come on and get in."

We do as we're told, first Tiffany and then me. No fighting over why neither of us gets to sit in the front seat. No Mom telling us it doesn't matter because we're all going to the same place any old way. No words at all. We leave, as still and quiet as the night.

Three

I remember the night before Dad left. We'd been living in Cedar Hills for months, and he'd come home from work, smiling and laughing, sometimes kissing Mom on the lips in front of Tiffany and me. For months he had nothing negative to say and then suddenly one day, something came up. It always started with something. This time it was sunlight.

"There is a pall over this house," Dad said.

"A 'pall'?" Mom asked. It was dinnertime. She paused, her fork halfway to her mouth.

"*Pall.* Something that covers and produces an effect of gloom," I said.

"Exactly. Look around you." Dad pointed with his knife. "We've got every light on, and it's still dim in here. Sun's not even down yet, and look at all the shadows. These dark walls. It's like living inside a coffin."

"We can repaint," Mom said.

"Let's paint the walls purple!" Tiffany shouted. If it

were up to her, the whole world would be the color of grape soda.

"Purple's too dark," Mom said. "What about a buttery yellow? Or sky blue? Bring the outside in?" She leaned forward in her chair, as though sitting on the edge of a cliff. As though if Dad said no to a new paint color, she'd pitch forward and fall. "Yes" would bring her back from the edge.

We had been in the Cedar Hills, New Jersey, apartment for almost eight months, longer than we'd stayed in the two before it. Mom had even unpacked everything. She'd never done that before. She usually unpacked what we needed—clothes for the season, silverware—and left everything else in boxes. But when we'd been in the apartment for six months, she unpacked the pictures and hung them along the hallway wall. By the time Dad started to talk about sunlight, the boxes had been broken down, tied up, and left outside for recycling.

"It's an issue of warmth," Dad said, more to himself than to us. "Can't even feel the heat half the time."

We could hear it, though. The radiators worked overtime, clanging, banging, and burping up steam, but I still had to wear my gray hoodie inside when the temperature outside went below sixty degrees.

"So, we bundle up, learn to adjust," Mom said quickly. She grabbed her water glass and raised it in a toast. "To learning to adjust."

We clinked glasses, everyone except Dad, who said, "Florida," and slapped his hand down flat on the dining room table.

"That's where Mickey lives!" Tiffany cried.

"Yes!" Dad said. "And you know what else Florida's got?" He looked at Mom, who looked down at her plate. We'd gone from Newburgh, New York, to Wilmington in favor of Delaware's cheaper rent, and from Delaware to Philadelphia because Dad wanted to see more black and brown faces, and then to Cedar Hills, New Jersey, where Dad had been certain we would stay.

"Florida's got summertime, all year round." He laughed. "I can see it now. I'll go on ahead and get a job working outside, independently. Wouldn't have to answer to anyone."

"Is that what this is about?" Mom asked.

That's what it had been about when we left Philadelphia. Mr. High-on-His-Horse Helmond, who ran the autobody shop, had called Dad something that meant he had to quit on the spot, pack up the car that day, and move us to Cedar Hills.

Dad went on as though he hadn't heard Mom. "I'd find us a place a few miles from the beach, maybe in Miami. A new place for the Aggregate, with palm trees in the yard. What do you say, Treasure?"

That's what Dad called the four of us, an aggregate, a whole formed by blending different elements. I leaned forward in my seat, giving Dad 100 percent of my attention and shutting out Mom's scrunched-up face.

"Let's go," I said.

"Yeah, let's go!" Tiffany said.

"Enough! We're not moving to Miami!" Mom yelled. "It's expensive, and we can barely afford to live *here*." She stared at Dad as if she didn't recognize him. "I can't believe you're doing this again. I just can't. You're—" She stopped, shook her head.

Dad's voice dropped low. "Go on, Lisa, tell me what I am."

Mom said nothing.

Dad slammed his hand on the table again, but this time there was no joy in it. I jumped. Tiffany jumped. The silverware on the table jumped too.

"You're a dreamer and a coward who can't face the reality of his own life," Mom said, and hate erupted inside of me like lava. Tiffany started banging her feet against her chair. *Thwack, thwack, thwack.* Mom pressed on, relentless. Dad taught me that word too.

"So you'd just go down ahead of us, get this outside job, set up house, and send for us when you're ready, huh?"

Dad nodded.

"Of course," Mom said. She stood and carried her plate to the kitchen. She was always telling us we had to take at least five bites of whatever was on our plates. Even if it was spider legs and fish tails. That night it was chicken, mashed potatoes, and collard greens. I wasn't sure Mom had taken even two bites.

She stood at the sink. "You know what I think?" she said.

"No," said Dad quietly. "But I'm sure you're gonna tell me."

"I am." Mom whirled around. "I think you'll go to Miami to set up house and we'll never hear from you again."

A feeling rose in my throat like I was trying to swallow a pill without water.

"That's not true, is it, Dad?" I asked.

"Is it?" Tiffany chimed in. Her eyes were big and shiny as half dollars.

After a pause, Dad said, "Of course it's not true. Your mama's just talking crazy because . . . Well, why are you, Lisa?"

"It's not me who's crazy," Mom said, and then there was a silence so thick it felt like you had to wade through it. I couldn't stand it. I cleared my throat.

"Do you need your inhaler?" Mom asked.

I shook my head.

Dad got up from the table and went to sit on the living room couch. I followed. Tiffany hesitated, but she came at last and climbed into Dad's lap. I had to settle for sitting beside him. I rested my head on his shoulder. We didn't say anything while Mom cleared the table. I listened to

Dad breathe, evenly at first, then harder through his nose, until at last he heaved a great sigh.

"Up," he said, and climbed out from beneath us.

He started for the door.

"You act like we're a burden to some other life you want to live," Mom said to his back.

He didn't answer. I knew where he was going: downstairs to sit on our building's back stoop. Dad turned. His eyes and shoulders seemed to droop as he stared at the three of us. As if we truly were too heavy for him to bear.

"I'm just trying to find the right place for us," he said. "The perfect place."

I believed him.

Four

MOM pulls onto the parkway and jerks the Explorer into the center lane. She leans on the driver's-side door, staring straight ahead. The road rumbles beneath us, and I wonder about the other people out driving tonight. People coming, people going, just like us. Only I have no idea where we're headed or when we'll get there.

"Where are we going?" I ask.

"For God's sake, Treasure, don't start with the questions already. I need to get my head together first."

My mind starts whirring. I tick off on my fingers all the places we could go.

Dad sister's house in Minnesota, but Mom called Aunt Ruby a month after Dad left to see if he'd gone to her house, and Aunt Ruby said, "Of course he's not here." And then she added, "What is it about you that my brother keeps running away from?" Mom recounted this conversation to me, word for word, and then called Aunt Ruby, Dad, and his entire side of the family a bunch of words she made me swear never to repeat.

Mom's aunt Grace has a place down south somewhere, but Mom and Dad haven't visited her since Mom was pregnant with Tiffany and I was four. According to Dad, when they got to Great-Aunt Grace's house, there was a note on her front door that said, "Locked up. Local jail. Bring money." After bailing Great-Aunt Grace out, Mom and Dad spent the next two days at her house, where Great-Aunt Grace spent nearly every waking moment asking Dad when he planned to get himself together. Dad vowed never to go back.

I have ticked off two places we can't go. There aren't any left.

We have nowhere to go.

The realization hits me like a punch to the chest, and for a moment, I can't breathe. I reach into my pocket for my inhaler and take two puffs. My breathing slows, but my mind does not.

Tiffany lifts her head from my lap. "Why can't we just go back? I wanna go back."

"No going back," Mom says.

"But what about Rachel and Wednesday tea parties?" Tiffany whines. "And who's gonna help Sam feed her hermit crabs?"

"It's over, all of it, Tiffany, and you can thank your father for that."

Tiffany buries her face in my lap again. It's not long before I feel her hot tears on my legs. A lump forms in my throat. I close my eyes and swallow hard. Mom slams on the brakes, and my eyes snap open. She lays into the horn and bangs her hand on the steering wheel.

"He can't do this to me!" she shouts. Tiffany sits up and looks at me, her face streaked with tears and snot. "Can't just up and leave me with two kids and no money."

Mom presses on the gas, almost kissing the bumper of the car in front of her until the driver gets the hint and moves out of her way. We pass a sign that says the speed limit is 55 miles per hour. I can tell Mom is going much faster than that.

"Maybe we should slow down," I suggest.

"Are you a state trooper now, Treasure?" she snaps. Then she sighs and says, "I'm sorry. I'm sorry about the dictionary, too, and about your friends, Tiffany, but it's not my fault. You know that, right? You know whose fault this is, don't you?"

Tiffany curls up in a ball beside me. "I'm hungry," she says.

"I wouldn't be doing this—any of this—if your father hadn't left me high and dry. I swear to God—"

"Mom," I cut in. "Tiffany said she's hungry."

Mom glances at us in the rearview mirror. "Okay. Fine. Let's get something to eat, then."

Mom pulls into the right lane, looking for something

to eat along the highway. We pass a Popeyes and an Olive Garden, both closed. It's after eleven o'clock at night. She gets off a few exits past the mall and drives around until we find a Gas & Grab, or As & Gab, if you go by the letters that still light up. Dad took us to the Gas & Grab over by our old apartment a few times. He always let Tiffany get a hero sandwich that was too big for her to finish, which is why she marches right up to this Gas & Grab's sandwich station and starts punching her order into the machine. Mom orders two more six-inch subs, totaling $15.56. Then she pulls out the credit card she uses only in emergencies, the rainy-day card. She lets Tiffany swipe it.

Declined.

"There was money on this a week ago," Mom says. She takes the card from Tiffany and swipes it again. Declined. She rubs the spot between her eyes. The man behind the deli counter looks up at us and then back down at his magazine. He probably didn't feel like making our sandwiches anyway.

"Come on, let's get something cheaper," Mom says.

"But I—" Tiffany says.

"I said, come *on.*"

Tiffany stomps her foot. "Daddy always lets me have a sandwich."

"Well, your father isn't here, is he? Now, let's go." Mom walks away, her head down and her shoulders hunched.

I follow her. We make it to the racks of chips before I

realize that Tiffany is not with us. I turn. She's still standing by the sandwich machine, her hands balled up in fists, her mouth open wide as the entrance to the Holland Tunnel. She lets out a wail that could shatter glass.

Mom runs over to grab her, but Tiffany bends at the waist and pulls back, all the while howling, "I want Daddy!" over and over again, until the words don't sound like words anymore. Not letting go of Tiffany's hand, Mom reaches into her back pocket and pulls out a wad of cash. She hands it to me and says, "Grab something." Then she picks Tiffany up and carries her out of the store, leaving me behind with eleven dollars in singles and the sandwich guy, who peers at me over the counter, shrugs, and says, "The sandwiches here suck, anyway."

I buy a big bag of chips, three cans of soda, and some Peanut M&M's. The cashier hands me back $4.27 in change, and as I stare at it nestled in the palm of my hand, panic grabs me by the throat. What if this is all the money we have left?

"Is it all right?" the cashier asks.

No. Nothing about our lives is all right. The cashier points at the change. "Is it all there?"

I nod and leave the store.

Five

WHEN I get back to the car, Tiffany is curled up in the back seat. She's not wailing, but she's not done crying, either. Mom is sitting beside her, holding Mr. Teddy Daniels.

"Okay, so, Mr. Teddy D. was walking down the street," Mom says. "Look, Tiffany, look at him walking." Tiffany raises her head. Mom makes Mr. Teddy D. hop across the seat. It's all wrong. Only Dad knows how to do it right.

"That's not how he's supposed to walk. He's a bear, not a bunny," Tiffany says.

"O-kay." Mom adjusts Teddy's hop to a more suitable walk. "So, he's just walking along when he comes upon this pile of poop."

"*No.* He's not supposed to *see* the poop," Tiffany whines. She covers her face with her hands and starts crying all over again. "I. Want. Daddy."

"All right, Tiffany," Mom says, stroking her hair, but

Tiffany is too far gone to stop now. "It'll be all right, Tiff-Tiff," Mom says, louder now, her voice laced with panic. It's still no use. Tiffany's wails fill up the car until Mom squeezes her eyes shut and shouts, "Look, Tiffany, we'll find him, all right? We'll find Daddy."

Tiffany sucks in a deep, shuddery breath. "We will?"

"Yes."

"How?" I ask.

"I'll figure something out," Mom says. "Lord knows he's not gonna get away with leaving me like this." She reaches for the door handle. "Come back here and cheer your sister up. I need to make a phone call."

I climb into the back and pry Mr. Teddy D. out of Tiffany's death grip.

"So," I say, "one day Mr. Teddy D. was walking down the street."

I make him look like he's walking the way Dad does, the tips of his tattered plaid feet skimming the seat. Tiffany watches him, quiet now.

"He was just walking along, whistling. Doo-dee-doo-dee-doo." I say this last bit in a high-pitched voice because I can't whistle. Tiffany doesn't seem to mind.

"He didn't even see it: a big old brown glob of poop. Doo-dee-doo-dee-doo—whoops! He slipped right in that poop and up he went. *Splat!*"

I make Mr. Teddy D. soar up in the air and land flat on

his back. Tiffany sniffles, a smile tugging at the corners of her mouth. She lives for the moment when he falls in that poop.

"Again," she whispers.

I run through Mr. Teddy Daniels's skit four more times before Tiffany cracks a smile. Not quite a standing ovation, but I'll take it. I climb into the front seat and Tiffany follows, planting herself firmly on the armrest, just as Mom gets into the car. She leans back in her seat and runs her index finger down the part in her hair. I want to ask her who she called and will they help us find Dad, but I don't.

"I'm still hungry," Tiffany says.

I hand her the bag of snacks and she goes right for the Peanut M&M's and a can of Sprite.

Mom watches her. "Didn't you get anything besides junk?" she asks me.

I shake my head.

"They had fruit cups in that fridge in the far corner."

"I didn't see them. I can go back in and—"

"It's too late now," Mom says as Tiffany tears open the M & M's. I reach into my pocket and hand Mom the change.

She doesn't count the money. She just balls it up in her hand.

"Is that it?" I ask.

"Is what it?"

"Nothing. Never mind."

We sit in the parking lot, not talking, the silence heavy and uncomfortable, like a coat I can't shrug off.

"Mom," I say, but she holds her free hand up, palm out, and says, "Just give me a minute to figure this out."

In the end it is more than a minute before she mutters, "It's the only way," and puts on her seat belt. Tiffany climbs into the back and buckles up. I strap myself in next to Mom. Mom dumps the change into the cup holder, turns the car on, and puts in her old-school-jams CD. Billie Holiday fills the car, crooning, *"Baby, won't you please come home"* in a voice like worn leather. We've heard this song a thousand times. Mom taps her fingers on the steering wheel in time with the rhythm, and Tiffany almost drowns Billie out, singing at the top of her voice in falsetto.

Mom puts the car in drive and pulls back out onto the highway. A million questions tug at my mind, but Tiffany is smiling now and we're going to find Dad, just like Mom said. So I sing along with Billie and keep myself from asking Mom how we're going to do that with three-quarters of a tank of gas and four dollars and twenty-seven cents.

Six

I fall asleep on some stretch of highway. When I wake up, the sun is up and we're on a road. A dirt road big enough for only two cars. The clock on the dashboard reads 5:46 a.m. The Explorer rocks us to and fro, rattling the change in Tiffany's Disney Fund. Tiffany sits up sleepily and asks, "Where are we?"

"I'm all turned around," Mom mutters. She pulls over to the side of the dirt road.

"All turned around where?" I ask, but Mom ignores me.

"If my memory serves me correctly," she murmurs to herself, "Iron Horse Road is . . ."

Mom throws the car into drive, as if she's suddenly figured something out. She makes a left at the next corner, and for a moment we're on a paved street. Then she turns again, and we're bumping along another dirt road.

"Is this Iron Horse?" she says, peering into the rear-view mirror. "I didn't see a street sign or anything. Did you?"

"Who lives here?" I ask. "Is this the country?"

"It's not really *country* country," Mom says, and slams on the brakes as a woman darts across the road in front of her. The woman's wearing a long flowered housedress and a big sun hat, and carrying a stack of papers.

"Is that lady crazy?" Tiffany asks.

"*Country* crazy," I answer. "Where are we, Mom?"

"Black Lake, Virginia."

"And who lives here?"

Mom sets her jaw. "Great-Aunt Grace."

"*What?* Why are we here?"

"I need money to find your father, don't I? Great-Aunt Grace owns her own store, which means she has money."

Tiffany pokes her head between our seats. "Is she the lady you make us talk to every Christmas, the one who sounds like a man on the phone?" she asks. "She calls me 'girl.' My name is Tiffany Onika Daniels, not girl. How would she feel if I called her 'old lady'?"

"Don't you dare," Mom says.

As we drive, we pass little boxes. You could call them houses if you were generous with the meaning of the word. They're all one-story and look like something Tiffany would draw. On the other side of the road is nothing but trees, thick and dark. Their leaves and branches throw spiked shadows on the road.

"Here we are," Mom says as she makes a sharp right. And now we're face-to-face with a green and white two-story house that looks like the victim of a serious beat down, with grubby aluminum siding and a porch screen with more holes than screen. Great-Aunt Grace may as well lay out a welcome mat for the mosquitoes.

The car comes to a halt, and Mom hauls herself out. Then she crosses to open the door on my side. The driveway isn't even paved. We've just pulled up onto the lawn.

"Let's get this over with," she says.

We stumble out, half blinded by the sun, and the heat hits every square inch of my body. It's humid in Jersey in July too, but this—this is like being on the inside of somebody's mouth.

"Okay," Mom says, as she crouches down until she's looking up at both of us. She's in full powwow mode. "Listen to me and listen good. Great-Aunt Grace does not tolerate nonsense, so from the minute you enter her house until the day you leave, you need to be on your best behavior and more grateful than you've ever been. Understood?"

"What do you mean, until the day we leave?" I ask.

"Understood?" Mom says again.

No, I don't understand, but Mom is already walking up to the house. She pulls open the screen door, crosses the porch to the front door, and rings the bell. "Get over here," she calls to us impatiently. Tiffany streaks across the lawn. She's on the porch in no time. I walk like I've got bricks strapped to the soles of my shoes.

Once I've joined them, Mom turns to us again. "When you see her, show her how happy you are to be here."

I will not show Great-Aunt Grace any such thing. In fact, I won't even look at her. I'm good at that, keeping my eyes on the ground. I will know her crumbling walkway and stairs, her shoes. I won't look up into her face, though, I vow. Not the entire time I'm in her presence.

But I do. Of course I do, the minute we ring the bell and she steps out onto the porch. She is tall and broad-shouldered, with big, thick-fingered hands and feet like stretch limos in black leather sneakers. It's as if God set out to make a mountain, changed his mind, and made a woman instead.

Dad told me how he and Mom went to the jail to pick her up that day eight years ago. They got there with a wad of tens and twenties and told the sheriff's deputy they were there for Grace Washington. He rocked back on his heels and said, "You really ought to leave her here. She's gone and stolen property from one of Black Lake's finest citizens. That woman is Public Enemy Number One." Dad said he thought about taking the deputy up on his offer, seeing as how Great-Aunt Grace had never liked him, but Mom wouldn't have it.

"Are you sure?" the deputy asked as he counted the money Dad had given him. "The town sure would appreciate it if she stayed here a while longer."

"We're sure," Mom snapped.

The deputy shook his head and went off to fetch Public Enemy Number One.

To hear Dad tell it, Great-Aunt Grace came strolling out of lockup with one hand in her pocket and a cigarette dangling from her mouth. She was taller than the deputy and almost as tall as Dad, but that didn't stop her from looking Dad over from head to toe. She said, "I see she hasn't left you yet." Then she looked at me and said, "So this is that little girl you been tellin' me all about, huh, Lisa? Let's pray she grows into that head."

"Surprise!" Mom shouts now. Great-Aunt Grace doesn't so much as raise an eyebrow and she doesn't say a thing. The silence stretches like a canyon between us, and Mom starts filling it with words.

"So, I probably should've called first, I know, but we're in a bit of a crisis. Darryl left again, and I have absolutely no idea where he went but I'm going to find him except I have no money and two girls to take care of and — here they are!" Mom sounds completely delirious. She nudges Tiffany and me forward. Tiffany, wide awake now and always ready for a close-up, smiles up at Great-Aunt Grace like a fool.

Great-Aunt Grace does not smile back. Instead she takes a pack of cigarettes from her shirt pocket, pulls one out, and lights it. She stares down at us through a cloud of smoke, her eyes sweeping over us like a searchlight. "Gonna be a storm," she says.

Seven

THERE is a storm. Its name is Grace Washington, and she rains down on Mom with questions and judgments in a voice like thunder.

"You lost your mind, Lisa? You could've called first."

"I know. I'm sorry, but I need help."

"You sure enough do. Can't just show up on somebody's doorstep at six in the dang mornin' with all this baggage." Our stuff is still in the Explorer. The baggage Great-Aunt Grace is talking about is Tiffany and me, but why? We're here only till she hands Mom some money.

Great-Aunt Grace shakes her head. "So, that no-'count man left you again, huh?" she says.

"Yes, he did."

"And you gonna find him?"

Mom nods.

"But you said you ain't got no money, didn't you?"

"Yes."

"And what about these kids?"

Mom says nothing when she should be saying something, so I do the talking for her. "We're going with her. Aren't we, Mom?"

Mom's eyes are on the porch floor. Wood painted white, dirty and scuffed in most places. There is an ashtray overflowing with cigarette butts on the table and a plastic wastebasket filled to the brim with trash. Does she really intend to leave us here?

"Mom?"

Great-Aunt Grace is looking at Mom too, waiting for an answer. Her eyes narrow to slits. She hasn't even offered to let us in her house or suggested we have a seat on her porch. Instead she points at her screen door and says, "You two, go around back and dig in the dirt or somethin'. Your mama and I got thangs to discuss. And don't let me find out you standin' down there on the side, listenin'."

"But—" I start up.

Great-Aunt Grace cuts me off, her voice like a shove in the back. "I said, go on, girl, *git.*"

Tiffany and I hurry down the porch steps, around the side of the house, and into Great-Aunt Grace's backyard, which is nothing but a sea of fenced-in grass with a rundown little shed plopped in the center of it. I take a seat on Great-Aunt Grace's back stoop. Tiffany lies down on the lawn, waving her arms and legs up and down, making grass angels.

"It's kind of pretty here," she says.

I can hear my hair frizzing. What I can't hear is what Mom is saying to Great-Aunt Grace.

"What if you had to stay here longer than today? Would you freak out?"

Tiffany sits up, mulling over my question. "Freak is a bad word. How long is longer?"

"I don't know, just longer."

"I guess I'd be okay, so long as you and Mom stayed too. You guys would stay too, right?"

I shrug. It's not my job to tell Tiffany that Mom is about to dump the two of us in Black Lake for who knows how long. Besides, I'm still holding out hope that I'm wrong. Tiffany goes back to making grass angels, and I think about how, if Dad were still around, none of this would be happening. Is he making his way to Florida right now, to find that perfect place for us? I bet that place isn't at all like Black Lake, with its boxy houses, bumpy dirt roads, and great-aunts who refuse to take out the trash.

The door opens behind me, and Mom pokes her head out. "Treasure, come here for a minute, will you?"

I join Mom just inside the kitchen, and I can tell just by looking at her face that she's already made up her mind.

"Are you *serious?*" I shout.

"It's only going to be for two weeks—three, tops."

"Three weeks!" I stomp my foot. I'm too old to act like this, but I don't care.

"Keep your voice down and stop with the feet." Mom

peers through the glass door at Tiffany, who is still sprawled in the grass. She places her hands on my shoulders. "Look at me, Treasure. Look at me."

I do. Her face glistens with sweat, and there are dark circles under her eyes.

"I need you to be a big girl about this and look after your sister while you're here, okay? Can you do that?" She gives me a little shake.

I shrug, more to get Mom's hands off my shoulders than anything else, and I stare at Great-Aunt Grace's floor. When I look up at Mom, there are tears clinging to her eyelashes.

"It won't be so bad, you'll see, and when I come back with Dad, we'll leave. Okay?"

I don't nod or say okay. Mom sniffles and wipes her eyes with the straps of her tank top. "I'm going outside to tell your sister now. Go out to the front and talk with your great-aunt."

"Talk with her about what?"

"I don't know. Think of something," Mom says, and goes out to the backyard.

I look around Great-Aunt Grace's kitchen. Everything in it looks old and worn—the sink, the fridge, the stove. There's a closet adjacent to the back door. I peek inside to find an ancient washer and dryer. I can't believe Mom is making us stay here. It's like we've traveled back in time.

I find Great-Aunt Grace still standing on the porch,

her hands in her pants pockets. I stay as far away as I can and say, "How old is this house anyway?"

"Built in 1874."

"I can tell." I wipe away a bead of sweat forming on my brow. "It is unnecessarily hot down here."

"All these years and I hadn't noticed." Great-Aunt Grace looks me over. "I see you still ain't grown into that head."

"My father says my head is fine."

"And you look just like him too—his face is all over yours. Your sister got lucky: she looks like a Washington through and through."

"There's nothing wrong with the way me or my dad looks."

"No, but there's sure enough something wrong with the way your daddy *is*. Can't tell your fool of a mother that, though. She's just like her mama, God rest my sister's soul, don't know herself outside the man she's with."

I ball my hands into fists. I want to hit Great-Aunt Grace, kick her in both shins, but I can't move. Can barely speak. "My mom knows who she is. She's part of an aggregate."

"A *what*?"

"A group, a collective—Dad, Mom, Tiffany, and me. The best aggregate there ever was."

Great-Aunt Grace raises an eyebrow. I hear Tiffany holler all the way from the backyard, "That's not fair!"

"Seems to me like you're more of a trio these days," Great-Aunt Grace says.

"But we're going to fix that."

"That's not fair, Mom. I don't wanna stay here without you!"

"And what if you can't?"

"I have to pee."

"The bathroom is down the hall past the living room, first door on your right."

I don't really have to pee. I stand at the sink and splash cold water on my face until it stops burning, until I can shake Great-Aunt Grace's words from my head.

I find Mom, Tiffany, and Great-Aunt Grace in the living room. Tiffany is sniffling but not on the brink of another meltdown, and Mom looks like she's just run ten miles in the Black Lake heat. Great-Aunt Grace is sitting in a brown armchair. She gestures to her couch, where Mom and Tiffany are already perched. "Sit."

I join them, but just barely. It's a miracle that the four of us can even fit in Great-Aunt Grace's living room, what with all the junk she's got crammed into it. There's unfolded laundry on the couch we're sitting on and piled-up newspapers on the coffee table beside it. Some of them are yellow with age. The figurines and furniture are coated with grime that seems to be a natural part of them, like moss on a rock.

The first sneeze sneaks up on me like a bully in the schoolyard.

"A-choo!"

My whole body jerks.

"A-choo! A-choo! A-choooo!"

I try to cover my mouth, but the sneezes are mini-explosions bursting out of me. By the time I'm done, the palm of my hand is covered with all kinds of nastiness and my eyes are watering something serious.

I'm going to die here.

"No, you're not," Mom says quickly.

Did I say that out loud?

I look up to see Great-Aunt Grace glaring at me. Guess I did. Oh, well.

"I'm going to die here," I say again.

Mom turns to Great-Aunt Grace. "She's not." She turns to me. "You're *not.*"

And she gives me a look that says, *Please, please,* please *keep your mouth shut.*

I wipe my nose on the neck of my T-shirt. Everyone is staring at me now, including Great-Aunt Grace. I stare right back.

"So, here you two are, in the flesh. Treasure and Tiffany," she says.

"And this is Mr. Teddy Daniels," Tiffany says, holding up her bear.

She was never any good at feeling out a situation.

Great-Aunt Grace shoots Tiffany a look that could turn her and Mr. Teddy D. into ash. Tiffany sniffles and looks down at her sneakers and sea-green socks. I realize now that the initials of Great-Aunt Grace spell *GAG*. And that she doesn't have a tooth in her head. Her mouth looks like a bottomless pit.

"So you're definitely okay with the girls staying for a bit?" Mom asks.

"I reckon I am, but for a short while. And I do mean short, Lisa. They just better keep their hands off my figurines." For some reason she looks at Tiffany when she says this. Tiffany's still looking down at her shoes and sea-green socks. "I've only got one other bedroom, so if y'all don't want to share, someone will be bunkin' in here with Mr. Shuffle."

She nods at the far corner of the living room. There, amid the clutter, lies the biggest black cat I've ever seen, spread out on the carpet like an oil spill. Tiffany and I look back and forth from Great-Aunt Grace to Mr. Shuffle.

"Well, he don't shuffle much no more, as it were," Great-Aunt Grace says. "I'll show y'all to your room, but don't be expectin' no grand tour."

She starts out of the living room and we follow, turning left down the hall where the bathroom is. We go up a flight of stairs at the end of the hall and find another bathroom at the top. Great-Aunt Grace's room is right across from it. Tiffany and I will share the bedroom at the end of the hallway. That's still not far enough away from Great-Aunt Grace for me, but my only other option is to sleep outside.

The room has two twin beds with a night table between them. The carpet is blue. There are no pictures on the walls or cheery figurines on the nightstands. But there is a clock, which reads 6:24 a.m. Sleeping here will be like sleeping in a jail cell. A jail cell that smells like mothballs. At least this room is cleaner than the living room. One thing is missing, though.

"Where's the TV?" Tiffany asks, her eyes raking over the space. "There wasn't one in the living room either."

"Ain't got one. I didn't get this whip-smart sittin' in front of the TV all the Lord's day long. TV rots the brain, girl."

I don't know if it's the sad look on Tiffany's face that makes me do it, or my growing dislike of Great-Aunt Grace. But the words are out of my mouth before I can stop them. "Whip-smart, huh? Smart people know the difference between 'got' and 'have,' and that 'ain't' is not a word."

The room gets so quiet you'd think we were at a wake. Mom looks at me, wide-eyed and open-mouthed, her face saying what her mouth does not: *What did I tell you before we came inside?* Tiffany looks at me too. In awe, like she knows as well as I do that I'm seconds away from the end of my life.

Great-Aunt Grace takes a step toward me, and all the solid stuff in me turns to liquid. Just as I'm thinking about darting by her and out the door—how fast could she be?—she stops and points her finger at me like a gun.

"You's a sassy-mouthed thing. But let me tell you something, Miss Treasure. I've got decades on you. Seen more than you, done more than you, heard more than you. So, girl, you better watch your mouth, or me and you gonna dance. And I can guarantee who will be the winner."

Great-Aunt Grace doesn't raise her voice, but my face is on fire all the same. She stares at me long and hard, and even though I feel about six inches tall, I stare right back at her. Her eyes are black as the night sky and red around the edges. She's got this staring thing down. I look away first.

"Now the rules," Great-Aunt Grace says. "First off, I don't take no sass. I think we've established that. Rule Number Two: No noise after eight o'clock. Face like this takes years of rest to come by."

Great-Aunt Grace's face has more lines than a crossword puzzle. But I've learned my lesson. I keep my mouth shut.

"Rule Number Three: Clean up behind yourselves. I ain't a maid."

Great-Aunt Grace reaches into her bulging shirt pocket and pulls out her pack of cigarettes. She bangs it against the palm of her hand. "That should just about cover it. Y'all get some sleep. When you get up, I'll have breakfast on the table."

She turns to leave, but not before fixing me with one last glare hot enough to burn a hole through my face.

Eight

MOM is on me quicker than fast. "What's wrong with you? Are you *trying* to tick her off?"

"It's not my fault she's a misanthrope."

"She isn't a misanthrope." Mom massages her temples. "What is that, anyway?"

"A person who hates other people."

"She doesn't hate anyone. She's just not one for company."

"She's mean. I'm going to call her Gag. G.A.G—Great-Aunt Grace. Get it?"

"You'd better not," Mom says.

"She is mean," Tiffany agrees. "I smiled at her, and she didn't even smile back at me. And I'm adorable. Ms. Regmont from 3F said so."

"Ms. Regmont has two hairless cats," I say.

"So?" Tiffany says.

"So I'm not sure she has the best handle on the concept of adorable."

Tiffany's hands fly to her hips. "Are you saying I'm not cute?"

"For the love of God," Mom mutters. "You're cute, Tiffany, okay? Jesus, Treasure, are you trying to get on everyone's bad side?"

I don't answer. I just stand right where I am, my arms crossed over my chest. "Gag's a criminal. How do you know she won't turn us on to a life of crime?"

"Don't be ridiculous. And *don't* call her Gag," Mom says.

"She has a million and seven rules." I have rules too, but that's my business. "Gag's rules are just oppressive. She's an oppressor!"

Mom sighs. "Okay, Treasure. I'm going to get your things out of the car. Try not to be too oppressed while I'm gone."

What I do is start planning our escape. By the time Mom comes back with two suitcases in one hand and my asthma machine in the other, I've got it almost figured out. When she returns from her second trip, this time carrying Tiffany's Disney Fund, I'm ready to state my case.

"Mom, our stay here is going to be detrimental to my health. First of all, Great-Aunt Grace smokes. And I don't think I need to remind you, my mother and current sole guardian, that smoking is bad for my asthma. Asthma, which—by the way—is aggravated by irritants, such as pet dander, dust, pollen, *and* cigarette smoke. Her house has all of those things, except maybe pollen. I believe you saw what just happened to me in the living room. I'll be lucky if I even survive this."

Mom takes the heavy blanket off of Tiffany's bed and folds it up. She tries to act like what I'm saying doesn't bother her, but she stops suddenly and presses down on the bridge of her nose with her fingertips. She helps Tiffany remove her sneakers and socks. Tiffany climbs into bed in her shorts and T-shirt, still holding on to Mr. Teddy D. Mom rubs her back and talks quietly to her about how things will be different once she finds Dad. We will convince him to stay for good this time, she says, just wait and see. Mom says "We," but she's leaving the two of us here with Great-Aunt Grace.

I go over to the other bed, the one closest to the window overlooking the front yard, but I don't sit down. Sunlight pours through the dingy glass and spills onto the blue comforter, revealing its frayed edges and three holes. When Tiffany falls asleep, Mom comes over to my side of the room.

"Sit down, Treasure," she says, and when I don't, she places her hands on my shoulders and pushes me down. "Take off those sneakers."

I use the toe of one to pull off the other, not bothering to untie the laces.

"Don't you care that my death is imminent if I stay here?"

"You have your nebulizer and your asthma pump, and before I leave I'll talk to Great-Aunt Grace about her smoking and her cat." Mom sounds like that conversation is the last one on earth she'd like to have.

"That's not going to change the fact that she hates me."

"She does not hate you. Where are you getting that from?" Mom bends to push my sneakers up against the nightstand. "And for the last time, Treasure, I'm only doing this because I have to."

Mom comes to sit down on the bed beside me. She looks worn out; the lines around her eyes and mouth seem deeper than ever. We drove more than six hours to get here, and now she's about to hit the road again to find Dad.

"But how?"

"How what?"

"How are you going to find him?"

"The rainy-day credit card. I haven't used mine in months, and a few weeks ago there was money on it. Now there's not, which means Dad must've used it. So I called and checked and found out where."

"And?"

"He used it at a Kmart in some town in North Carolina, Boydon, I think, and at a convenience store there too. So I'm going to go down there with the pictures in my wallet and ask around, see if anyone has seen him. Great-Aunt Grace says this is the dumbest idea she's ever heard. I say desperate times call for desperate measures."

"How desperate are we?"

"We have nowhere else to go."

Whenever we moved with Dad, he always had the next place set up for us. He'd have made some calls or skipped work to fill out a rental application, and Mom would be mad at first, but in the end she'd shake her head and say, "This is what I get for falling in love with a crazy, restless man." Dad isn't here now, and what if Mom can't find him in the next two weeks? Will we be stuck staying with Great-Aunt Grace?

"You have to take us with you. We could help you look."

Mom gets to her feet. "No. It's better for you girls to stay here. I'll call as much as possible and I'll see you soon, okay?" Mom leans down to plant a cold-lipped kiss on my cheek. She reaches into her pockets and pulls out money. She puts it on the nightstand beside me. "Here. You take this for emergencies. I'm getting cash from Grace." And then she's gone, shutting the door softly behind her. I lie down on my raggedy bed and close my eyes.

It was Dad's idea to name me Treasure. Treasure Jeanie May Daniels. He says he gave me that name because that's what I was to him and Mom, a treasure. Something they wanted to cradle in their hands and protect from the world.

But people don't leave treasures behind, not for two months or even for two weeks.

First Dad. Now Mom.

I'll go by Jeanie until they both come back.

Nine

I wake up to the sound of Tiffany in the middle of a throat-ripping wail. It takes me a while to rub the crust out of my eyes and remember where we are. At Great-Aunt Grace's house in Black Lake, Virginia, where Tiffany's sitting on the bedroom floor tearing through her suitcase. Mr. Teddy Daniels lies crumpled at her feet.

"They're not in here!" she hollers. "Mom didn't pack them!"

"Take it easy, Tiffany," I whisper. All this racket is bound to bring Great-Aunt Grace up here, and the last thing I want is to see her face—or hear her voice—any sooner than I have to.

Tiffany doesn't take the hint. "Mr. Teddy Daniels's clothes aren't in the suitcase!" she yells. "He *needs* them, Treasure!" She picks him up and clutches him to her heaving chest. "You said you saw her pack them. You *said!*"

"I know, but—"

"Liar!"

I go over and turn Tiffany's suitcase upside down, pawing through her cartoon-character panties and bright tops. Not a scrap of Mr. Teddy D.'s wardrobe to be found.

"Can't he just wear his overalls while we're here?"

Tiffany's eyes open wide. I should've known how stupid that question was before I asked it.

"Mr. Teddy Daniels can't wear the same clothes every day. He needs clean ones, just like you!"

The clock on the nightstand reads 8:52 a.m. I've slept for barely two hours. Now a new kind of tiredness hits me, one that spreads all over my body and makes my shoulders sag. I stare at the pile of clothes on the floor. A knot of anger forms in my stomach. Mr. Teddy Daniels's clothes are more important to Tiffany than her own clothes. How could Mom say she packed them when she didn't?

Tiffany's still wailing, and this time I know better than to run through Mr. Teddy Daniels's skit. Seeing her bear slip in invisible poop while wearing his same old overalls is not going to cheer her up. Still, I have to do something before—

The door flies open. "What's with all this noise?"

Great-Aunt Grace stands in the doorway, holding an unlit cigarette.

Tiffany's too involved in her hysterics to answer, so I do it for her. "Mom forgot to pack Mr. Teddy Daniels's outfits. He has one for every day of the week."

Great-Aunt Grace raises one eyebrow. "What in the

sweet name of Jesus does a stuffed animal need clothes for? Makes about as much sense as nonsmokin' establishments. Rule Number Four: No cryin' over foolishness. Now, y'all come get something to eat."

~~~~~~

Great-Aunt Grace can't cook. The pieces of bacon that aren't crispy and black are raw and floppy. There's no middle ground. I'm either going to get some kind of poisoning from eating undercooked pork or lose a tooth. She places something in front of me that looks like a bowl of spitballs.

My face must have asked a question because she answers, "Grits. By the time you get to the bottom of that bowl, you'll be a southerner through and through."

Grits: Rough, hard particles of stuff, like sand. And dirt. A word that should not be applied to food.

Great-Aunt Grace pushes a pat of butter toward me. "Makes 'em taste like heaven." Coming out of her toothless mouth, heaven sounds like the other place.

I mix the butter in the steaming grits anyway—yellow on white, like dog pee on snow. I stick a spoon in my grits and take just a small bite off the top. I roll them around in my mouth—and my taste buds turn against me. They like the buttery taste. I take another bite. The grits are sweet and lumpy and make me feel warm all the way to my pinky toes.

Tiffany picks at her food, her eyes on Mr. Teddy Daniels.

Great-Aunt Grace doesn't eat at all. She smokes the rest of her cigarette and flutters around us like a bad-tempered waitress. When Tiffany drops her spoon, Great-Aunt Grace is right there to give her a dirty look and hand her another. When I finish my orange juice, she pours me more so fast it's like she conjured the stuff out of thin air.

I watch Great-Aunt Grace's every move. She's got about twenty-nine strands of hair, pulled back off her face in a tiny bun. She has to be three hundred years old. Mr. Shuffle waddles in and she tosses him a piece of flabby bacon. He gulps it down in two bites, and Great-Aunt Grace tosses him another piece. When she catches me watching her, she says, "You got something you wanna say, Miss Treasure?"

"Actually, it's Jeanie."

"What?"

"I'm not going by Treasure anymore. I'd like to be called Jeanie now. It's my middle name."

"My middle name is Onika, but I'm still Tiffany, and this is still Mr. Teddy Daniels." Tiffany holds up her bear.

Great-Aunt Grace comes to stand over us at the table. "If y'all think I got time to be rememberin' middle names and teddy bear names, y'all got another think comin'." She looks right at me. "I'll call you whatever I want to, girl, and when I do, you best come runnin'. Understood?"

She stares, waiting for an answer. I nod.

"Can't hear you, girl."

"Yes, I understand," I say between clenched teeth.

"Good." Great-Aunt Grace eyes us, her forehead creased like she's deep in thought. "Y'all need chores," she says.

"Chores?" Tiffany asks, as if the word is foreign to her.

"Yes, chores. Didn't your mama and daddy put y'all to work?"

Tiffany and I shake our heads.

"Spoiled as the day is long, I see. Well, y'all gonna pull your weight while you're down here with me." Great-Aunt Grace points at Tiffany. "You gonna feed Mr. Shuffle every mornin' and every night. Half a cup of dry food and a can of wet. And don't take too long gettin' the food down, girl, or he'll swat you good. Lord knows he ain't got all day. Now you." Great-Aunt Grace jabs her index finger at me. "Starting tomorrow, you gonna wash the breakfast and dinner dishes."

"Dishes?" I say slowly. "Every day?"

"Every. Dang. Day. Now hurry up and finish eatin'."

I go back to eating my grits, slowly, so Great-Aunt Grace won't know I like them. I'm snail-walking the fifth spoonful to my mouth when the phone rings. Great-Aunt Grace says, "I'll-get-it-Treasure-stop-messin'-in-them-grits," all in one breath as she hurries by me.

Is it wrong to will an old lady to fall on a linoleum floor? In this case, no, it's not. But Great-Aunt Grace makes it to the phone in the living room without so much as a stumble. She tells whoever it is that she doesn't have time to talk because she's been invaded by her freeloading kin.

She returns to the kitchen a few minutes later and tells us it's time to go.

"The three of us got thangs to do," she says.

Great-Aunt Grace clears our plates away before either of us is finished. *Thangs?* What *thangs?*

"Hurry up, wash those faces and get dressed so we can get goin'."

"Going where?" Tiffany asks. "To do super-fun stuff like Mommy said?"

"Not even. Now, go upstairs and do like I told you."

Tiffany hurries past me and out of the kitchen.

We take our time, neither of us in a rush to find out what Great-Aunt Grace has planned for us. I find our toothbrushes in one of the suitcases and head down the hall to the bathroom, Tiffany trailing behind me. The upstairs bathroom is small and tiled in the same dull shade of blue as the carpeting. Must be Great-Aunt Grace's favorite color. There's a small window in here, overlooking her backyard.

"Mommy said Great-Aunt Grace might take us on adventures," Tiffany says, Crest foaming up at the corners of her mouth.

I spit a wad of toothpaste in the sink. "Does Gag seem like the type of person to go on adventures? She's three hundred years old."

"Mr. Putter is old, but he does fun stuff with his cat, Tabby, all the time," Tiffany replies. "Great-Aunt Grace has a cat, and Mommy told you not to call her Gag, Treasure."

"My name is Jeanie and I'll call *Gag* whatever I want."

"You're gonna be in big trouble if she hears you."

We hear Great-Aunt Grace's feet on the stairs. Tiffany and I go tearing out of the bathroom, down the hallway, and back to our room. We pull clothes from our suitcases, like we were up here getting dressed all along and not lollygagging in the bathroom.

Great-Aunt Grace appears in the doorway. "Movin' like molasses, I see. Well, that ain't gonna get you out of workin', so you best come on."

"*Working?* Where?" Tiffany asks.

"In my store, girl."

Suddenly I remember Mom saying that Great-Aunt Grace owns her own store. What does she sell? Cigarettes and burnt-up bacon?

"I'll tell y'all like I told your mama," Great-Aunt Grace goes on. "You two ain't gonna lay around doin' nothin' for the next two weeks after I done paid back rent and gave your mama money to chase behind your fool daddy. No, ma'am. Not on my watch."

"But we're already going to be doing chores," I say. Great-Aunt Grace is unmoved. "We're underage, you know. You could be violating child labor laws."

"And you're violatin' Rule Number Five: Tuck in your lips and do what I say."

Great-Aunt Grace fixes me with her death stare and goes to stand over Tiffany, who starts moving in fast-forward. She's dressed in no time. I hurry up and finish too. I don't want Great-Aunt Grace hovering over me like some geriatric vulture. Tiffany grabs Mr. Teddy Daniels; I grab my inhaler and some of the emergency money Mom gave me and shove them in the pockets of my shorts.

As she turns to leave the room, Great-Aunt Grace stumbles over Tiffany's three-gallon water bottle of change. She doesn't fall, but a small smile tugs at the corners of my mouth just the same.

"What's this?"

Tiffany answers in a small voice. "My Disney Fund. I'm going to Disney World one day."

"With nickels and dimes, girl?"

"There're eight dollar bills in there too!"

Great-Aunt Grace rolls her eyes and starts down the hallway. We follow her downstairs, where she stops in the kitchen to grab her things. Great-Aunt Grace doesn't carry a purse. She puts her keys and wallet in her pants pockets, picks up a small red cooler from the kitchen counter, and ushers us out the door in front of her.

It's even hotter now than it was before. Great-Aunt Grace starts up the walkway. I don't move. I look over at the patch of grass where the driveway should be. Empty save for a big bald space in the middle.

"Don't you have a car? Aren't you going to drive us?"

She looks at me like I've asked her if she wants to bend over and let Tiffany and me climb on her back.

"I don't drive. Besides, that won't be necessary. Moe and Joe will get us where we need to be."

"Who're Moe and Joe?" Tiffany asks.

Great-Aunt Grace points down at her two sneakered feet.

"We can't walk in this heat!"

Great-Aunt Grace swats away my words the way a horse swats flies.

I should take Tiffany and demand that Great-Aunt Grace let us back inside. But even this heat isn't enough to make me stupid. It's one thing to suggest to Great-Aunt Grace that walking in weather this hot is ridiculous. It's an entirely different beast to try to go back inside when she told us to come out. We have no choice but to follow her. This is going to be the Longest. Walk. Ever.

It is a bit after nine now, the butt crack of dawn in the summer as far as I'm concerned. And yet, people are out. Two old men wearing tank tops and shorts sit on the saggy porch of a white house. When a car drives past, they wave. They don't wave at us. In fact, they exchange a look and shake their heads. As we pass the house two doors down from Great-Aunt Grace's, a woman comes flying out the front door, carrying a stack of papers. It's the same woman who darted in front of Mom's car on our way here. She's still wearing her flowered housedress and big sun hat.

"Grace!" the woman calls out.

I stop. Tiffany does too. Great-Aunt Grace keeps on walking, her cooler banging against her thigh.

"Grace!" The woman comes charging down her walkway and stops beside Tiffany and me. She doesn't even acknowledge our presence. "I'm talking to you!" she shouts at Great-Aunt Grace's back.

"And that is unfortunate, Dot," Great-Aunt Grace says loudly, but she stops walking and turns to face the woman. There's a stretch of dirt road between Great-Aunt Grace and Dot that doesn't invite conversation, but Dot closes the distance in four huge steps.

"I've been robbed. Low-down dirty thief stole my elephant statue with the little flecks of gold in it. Look." Dot pulls a flier from the top of her pile and waves it in Great-Aunt Grace's face. Great-Aunt Grace reaches up with her free hand and snatches it.

"A hundred-dollar reward, huh?" she asks.

"Yes, indeed. I gotta get to the bottom of this!"

"What you *got* is too much dang free time," Great-Aunt Grace replies, crumpling up Dot's flier and shoving it in her pants pocket.

Dot's nostrils flare. "It's been nearly a decade, but don't think I forgot how you robbed my kin all those years ago. Would you happen to know anything about my missing statue?"

"Why would I?"

"Everyone knows you got a record, Grace, and a knack for getting yourself caught up in the worst type of situations."

"That explains me standin' here talkin' to you. Come on, girls, let's go."

Great-Aunt Grace strides away, leaving Tiffany and me to stare after Dot, who storms back to her house and slams the door shut behind her. Tiffany runs to catch up to Great-Aunt Grace. I do too, though neither of us walks close enough to rub elbows with her.

"Do you think someone broke in and stole Mr. Teddy Daniels's clothes?"

"Don't be ridiculous, girl. Your mama forgot to pack them."

Tiffany's face falls.

"Don't worry about it," I tell Tiffany. "When Mom comes back with Dad, we'll get more clothes for Mr. Teddy D."

"You promise?"

"Yes."

Tiffany smiles. Great-Aunt Grace rolls her eyes.

When we come almost to the end of Iron Horse Road, Tiffany furrows her brow and looks up at Great-Aunt Grace. "What kind of records do you have?"

"What, girl?"

"That lady said everybody knows you got records."

"She means a police record. It means Great-Aunt Grace has been arrested, right?" I say. "Mom and Dad got her out of jail."

"That's right, girl. Guess you're not as simple as you look."

But I bet she's as old as *she* looks. And maybe she's a thief on top of everything else.

"Did you get arrested for stealing?" I ask.

"Depends on how you see thangs. See, Dot's fool son was the mail boy back in the day, and he always used to come through here with this portable radio in his truck, blastin' that be-pop."

"You mean hip-hop?"

"Who's tellin' this story, girl, you or me?" Great-Aunt Grace snaps. "So he used to come through blastin' that be-pop, loud enough to make your dang ears bleed. I told him if you don't cut it out when you come round my house, I'm gonna give you what for. He came around next day, still blastin' that noise, but I was ready for him. Told him he had a flat rear tire. When he got out his truck to check, I reached in and took that dang radio."

"You stole some kid's radio?" Tiffany asks, incredulous.

"Threw it on the ground and smashed it too."

I can just picture Great-Aunt Grace out by her mailbox, waiting to strike.

"So did you take Dot's elephant, too?" I ask.

"Yeah, did you?" Tiffany chimes in.

"Dot's a fool. This town is full of 'em. Don't worry: Y'all will fit right in."

There are so many places Mom could've left us instead of with Great-Aunt Grace. An abandoned building, maybe, or the sewer. The Everglades. I'd rather take my chances with the gators and the snakes.

Ten

WE walk for what feels like a month. When we reach the end of Great-Aunt Grace's road, we turn down another and yet another, both almost identical to hers: narrow and flanked on either side by boxy, rundown houses. Soon we turn left and come to the street where Mom made her U-turn. Here there's a gas station, a convenience store, and two signs that we haven't completely fallen off the face of the earth: A few cars drive by and a woman passes us, jogging.

"Are we almost there?" Tiffany says.

"No, and whinin' ain't gonna speed us up, so cut it out, girl."

Tiffany clamps her mouth shut and scowls. We keep on walking until we come to a stoplight. We cross the street and now we're in what Great-Aunt Grace calls downtown Black Lake, which isn't much more than a few blocks with small stores on either side of the street, languishing in the shade of faded awnings. DeGroat's Dry Cleaning; W. T. Fine Arts and Prints; Pet and Purr.

Great-Aunt Grace's store is called Grace's Goodies. We're just stopping in front of its heavy metal-and-glass door beneath a worn burgundy awning when a voice calls out, "Morning, Ms. Washington."

A young man is climbing out of the driver's side of a shiny black pickup truck. He's broad-shouldered and the deep brown of milk chocolate. He has muscles on top of muscles and looks like he walked straight off the cover of one of Mom's urban romance novels, the ones Dad asked her to stop reading in public.

"Mornin', Byron," Great-Aunt Grace says.

"You're looking lovely as ever today," Byron says.

Great-Aunt Grace is sweaty and scowling. If that's lovely, I'd hate to see what Byron considers unpleasant. "Aren't you gonna introduce me to your pretty friends?"

My face grows hot. Tiffany smiles up at him. She loves anyone who calls her pretty.

"Not friends," Great-Aunt Grace says, setting her cooler down. "Family."

"Well, they got names?"

Before Great-Aunt Grace can answer, a girl comes bursting out of the store two doors down from Grace's Goodies, carrying a greasy brown paper bag. She's wearing the shortest shorts I've ever seen and a tank top thinner than one-ply toilet paper.

Byron holds his hand out for the paper bag and peeks inside. "You got me sesame seed."

"You asked for sesame seed, didn't you?"

"No. I asked for poppy."

The girl cocks her head to the side and looks at Byron, wide-eyed. "They're pretty much the same thing. But my manners!" She waves at Great-Aunt Grace, Tiffany, and me. "I'm Sasha, Byron's girl."

Great-Aunt Grace eyes the girl's wrists, which are covered in tangled gold bracelets. Sasha notices and holds her arms out so Great-Aunt Grace can get a closer look. "I'm a jewelry freak," she says.

Byron is scowling at her. She understands the look on his face, which says, plain as day, *Go get in the car,* because that's exactly what she does.

"Where'd you find that one?" Great-Aunt Grace asks.

"She lives over in Bracie." Byron smiles, showing two rows of perfect teeth. "You know I love the ladies. Listen, you beautiful girls have yourself a good day, you hear?"

"You too," Great-Aunt Grace says, fishing her keys out of her pants pocket.

"He said I'm beautiful," Tiffany says, as Byron pulls away from the curb.

"Girl, please," Great-Aunt Grace says. "That fool has more women than he has sense." She grabs her cooler, unlocks the door to Grace's Goodies, and ushers us inside.

The first things I see are the shiny wrappers of rows and rows of candy glittering in the murky light, like coins in a fountain. Great-Aunt Grace flicks a switch, and everything comes into sharper focus. Reese's Peanut Butter Cups, 3 Musketeers, Swedish Fish, Skittles, no-name chocolate bars (but who cares because chocolate is chocolate), sour watermelons, gummy bears. My eyes don't know where to settle and my hands don't know what to grab.

"Don't even think about askin' for anything."

My eyes land on Great-Aunt Grace. "I don't even like candy."

I would lie, cheat, and steal for candy. And the first chance I get, I'm going for a pack of Sour Patch Kids. In the meantime, Great-Aunt Grace informs us that there is work to be done. I'm to wipe down the shelves in the back, and Tiffany—

"Can I work the register?" she pleads.

Tiffany has a thing for buttons.

Great-Aunt Grace grunts, neither a yes nor a no. "First you're gonna help me restock the shelves out here in the front, make sure there's enough of everything."

Tiffany and I follow Great-Aunt Grace through a waist-high swinging door that's connected to the counter. As we pass the cash register, Tiffany looks back and sighs.

Great-Aunt Grace leads us to the stockroom, where I'll be working. It's cold and gray, but anything is better than being outside in the Black Lake heat. Shelves line each wall, and on each shelf are boxes and boxes of candy. When I turn to look toward the front of the store, it's like it's back in Jersey, it's so far away. Tucked away in the corner is a phone hanging on the wall. Does it work? Can I use it to call for help? It's not fair that Great-Aunt Grace won't let me work in the front too. She probably doesn't want to be around me any more than I want to be around her. On the plus side, working in the stockroom means I'll be left unattended with more candy than I'll probably ever see again.

It's like Great-Aunt Grace reads my mind.

"I know which boxes ain't open, and of the ones that are, I know exactly how much candy is in 'em." She gives me a long, hard look. "You want some, you gotta pay, just like everybody else."

I think about the money in my pocket. Mom gave it to me for emergencies. Somehow it doesn't seem right to spend any of it on candy—candy that should be free, any old way. And now that I know cleaning these shelves isn't going to produce any type of reward—given or otherwise—the shelves and boxes seem to multiply right before my eyes.

"I can't do this by myself."

"Maybe you won't have to."

"Maybe?"

"You might get help, you might not. Pray on it, girl."

Great-Aunt Grace takes a few rags and a bottle of yellow cleaner down from the shelf next to her and hands them to me.

I *might* get help? To do this job, I'm going to need the

help of ten men. Or Jesus. I hope Great-Aunt Grace doesn't plan on sending Tiffany to work back here. I can just picture her spindly arms trembling. Before I can ask Great-Aunt Grace about this possible help, she is on her way to the front. Tiffany turns and waves at me over her shoulder. I see pity in her eyes.

What if I spent all day sitting on this cold stockroom floor, not cleaning a single shelf? Would Great-Aunt Grace call Mom and tell her to come back and pick me up? Doubt it. She's more the warm-your-butt-with-a-whupping type.

I take one deep breath through my nose and let it out through my mouth. Then I get to work, pulling the boxes down from the first shelf. When it's empty, I start wiping it down.

I'm bored within minutes. The cleaner turns out to be pine-scented and slick. It leaves a greasy sheen on the shelf and I have to wipe extra hard to get it to go away. Which means my shoulders go first. Then my patience, followed by my will to live. I can hear Great-Aunt Grace explaining to Tiffany how the cash register works.

"You type in the price and hit this button. . . . No, not that one; this one, girl. It's like tryin' to teach Mr. Shuffle."

By the time I'm up on the ladder, cleaning the top shelf, I'm so deep into counting the many ways I despise my great-aunt, I don't even notice the witch herself standing below me.

"Girl, you deaf or something?"

I look down, right into Great-Aunt Grace's flared nostrils. A boy is with her. A boy around my age wearing khaki cargo shorts and an orange T-shirt with a robot on the front of it.

"Help is here," Great-Aunt Grace says. "Get on down here and meet him."

I climb down the ladder slowly. The boy looks at me and I look back at him. He has copper-colored skin and eyes the color of pencil shavings.

"This is Terrance. Terrance, this is Treasure. She wants to be called Jeanie, but you can ignore that nonsense. Terrance is new to town, just like you, but he don't talk back. You could learn a few things from him." Great-Aunt Grace runs her index finger over one of the shelves I've just cleaned. "He's gonna have to teach you a thing or two about cleaning my shelves, too."

"It's nice to meet you," Terrance says, holding out his hand. I stare at it like it has eight legs.

"Try to teach her some manners while you're at it," Great-Aunt Grace tells him.

The minute she leaves us to the shelves, that boy says, "So you're not into shaking hands? Don't worry. I'm not offended. Are you a germaphobe or something, though? My aunt is. She buys hand sanitizer by the bulk. Want some Pop Rocks?"

He reaches into his pocket and holds the box out to me. Pop Rocks aren't my favorite candy, but I can deal with them, especially the blue ones, which he has. But taking candy from Terrance might make him think we're friends, and I don't make friends. It's the first and most important of my Moving Rules: *Don't make friends. Avoid extended eye contact and turn down all invitations for play dates. Try not to smile. Don't waste words, which means no small talk. Try not to speak unless your life—or grades—depends on it.*

I shake my head, and Terrance shrugs. "More for me," he says, and I have to spend the next ten minutes listening to the Pop Rocks crackle in his mouth and not in mine.

Great-Aunt Grace's booming voice spills into the back as she talks with the customers who come in. One is a woman with a voice that could cut glass.

"Can you believe it? Scoundrel broke into the sheriff's house and stole Eunetta's pearls," the woman says. "Ain't that a cryin' shame?"

"Reckon it is," Great-Aunt Grace replies.

"I hear the sheriff and Eunetta are offering a reward to the man who finds the heathens responsible."

"Or woman."

"Right," the woman says slowly. "You got any more Juicy Fruit?"

"Last rack, top shelf," Great-Aunt Grace says, and then the two of them start talking about the new pastor at the church—"He's full of nothin' but hot air," says Great-Aunt Grace—and I turn my attention back to the shelves.

"My mama is real bothered by the break-ins," Terrance says. "Is there a lot of crime where you're from?"

What kind of question is that? I don't answer.

"I guess not. We moved here because my father got a job as the head of the zoology department at the University of Richmond. We're staying with my grandma until we find a house that meets my mama's standards."

Head of the zoology department? Terrance's family must have a gang of money. So what's he doing here, cleaning shelves with me? The question almost breaks free, but I clamp my lips shut and hold it in. Terrance keeps right on talking, moving on from the break-ins to his terrarium, the time machine he's planning on building, and his quest to find out what the special sauce on a Big Mac is made of. It's not Thousand Island dressing like everyone thinks, Terrance says. The ingredients are way more sinister than that.

For the next hour, conversation comes pouring out of him fast and unstoppable, like a waterfall. He doesn't stop even to swallow. Isn't his mouth getting dry? Or the back of his throat starting to itch?

"So, long story short, I mentioned the theory of evolution one too many times. Now my grandma is concerned with the state of my soul. That's why I decided to start doing volunteer work, to earn some Jesus points, you know? She told me to steer clear of Ms. Washington because she's different in a bad way."

Great-Aunt Grace is just bad. Period.

"But I like a challenge, you know? Besides, Ms. Washington gives me free candy for helping out."

"Are you *serious?*"

Terrance jumps at the sound of my voice. "Um, serious about what?"

"The free candy."

"Yup." Terrance holds out the Pop Rocks as proof. "Don't you get free candy too? I mean, you're related and all. Anyway, do you want to hear a joke my dad's friend told me? He's an oncologist. All right, here goes. Knock, knock."

Silence.

"You're supposed to say, 'Who's there?' Okay, whatever. I'll say it. Who's there? Interrupting doctor." Terrance pauses. "Now *you* say, 'Interrupting doctor who?'"

He's staring at me expectantly, and I don't think he intends to stop until I play along. I spit out the words: "Interrupting doctor—"

"You have cancer."

Now it's my turn to stare at Terrance. He looks at his shoes, then up at me. "It's the cancer part, right? Society is just not ready to laugh about it. Maybe I should change it to 'You have tyrotoxism.' Poisoning by cheese. That's funny, right?"

"Let's just clean the shelves, okay?" I say.

"Okay, but first—what about this one? A guy walks into a bar with a zebra. Wait, no. It's a giraffe. Let me start over. So this guy walks into a bar with a giraffe . . ."

I close my eyes and grit my teeth.

Eleven

TERRANCE tells me all about how his father is off in Venezuela, studying huge tarantulas called Goliath bird eaters. He tells me what he'll name his cockatoo once his mother gives in and confronts her fear of birds—Clancy. By the time he starts talking about his allergy to pit fruits, I check out of the conversation and start flipping through the dictionary in my head, beginning with the A's.

Ameliorate: to make or become better; to make more bearable, as in, the only way to ameliorate my time with Terrance would be to glue his mouth shut.

I make it to *cacophony*—a harsh clash of sounds—when Terrance asks, "So is it just you and your sister visiting Ms. Washington? Where're your parents?"

My dad has been gone for two and a half months and my mom is driving around searching for him, using a credit-card bill as her guide. As if Terrance would understand, with his zoologist father and his mother with her high living standards. I bet they have dinner together as a family every night and the only time his father has ever left was for a business trip and even then he made sure to call every night.

The grits and bacon churn in my stomach. I close my eyes and press my forehead against the cool metal of the shelves.

"Are you okay?" Terrance asks.

"I'm fine."

"Are you—"

"I said I'm fine."

The clock above the stockroom door reads 12:10 when Great-Aunt Grace returns, carrying two aluminum-foiled bundles and two bottles of red juice. The bundle turns out to be a sandwich, turkey with mayo on white bread. She hands one to Terrance and the other to me. I wait for him to sit down near the door to the storage room. Then I pick a section of cold floor all the way on the other side of the room, far enough away from Terrance to discourage any further conversation, and open my sandwich. I've barely taken a bite when Tiffany waltzes in, carrying what's left of her own lunch. Her smile could span the equator.

"I rung up a customer," she yells, throwing herself down on the floor next to me. "It was a boy, and he bought seven loose Tootsie Rolls. I don't like Tootsie Rolls 'cause they make my teeth hurt. Anywho, it came to thirty-five cents and he paid with two quarters. Guess how much his change was?"

"Hmmm, I don't know. Twelve cents?"

"No!"

"Fourteen, then." I wipe mayo from the corner of her mouth.

"Noooo." Tiffany giggles. "Fifteen, silly. But I didn't even have to know because the cash register told me."

Tiffany will ask for a cash register for Christmas.

Great-Aunt Grace returns. She goes over to Terrance. What is she doing? Checking up on me? They come over to where I'm sitting, and Great-Aunt Grace says, "Seems to me you've worked hard enough today." She looks from Terrance to me, and there's something about the determined look in her eyes that I don't like one bit. "So I was thinkin' maybe the two of you could scoot off for a little, and Terrance here could show you around."

I'd rather clean every shelf with my tongue than be shown around by Terrance. I never knew a boy who could talk so much. I will suffocate under the weight of his endless conversation.

Terrance, on the other hand, is ready to go. He nods and smiles at me, his eyebrows finally doing what they've been threatening to ever since we were introduced: kiss his hairline.

"Maybe some other time," I say. "I don't like to leave a job unfinished."

"Girl, please," Great-Aunt Grace says. "Three hours and you've barely cleaned five shelves. Rate you goin', you be my age before you finish. Now, go on, git."

She says this in a way that makes me snap my mouth shut and get to my feet.

"What about Tiffany?" I ask weakly. She talks as much as Terrance, and with the two of them yakking, I won't have to talk to anyone.

But Tiffany shakes her head hard enough to make her braided ponytail smack her on each cheek. "The cash register needs me."

And that's that. Great-Aunt Grace all but shoves us out the door.

Now it's my turn to talk. "There's no need to show me around. I won't be here long."

"When you leaving?"

"Two weeks."

"Where you going?"

"Don't know."

"O-kaaaay."

I stop on the cracked sidewalk and face Terrance. "So you can stop trying to be my friend. I won't be around long enough for all that."

"Two weeks isn't that short of a time. Mayflies only live a day and they get a whole lot done. Mayflies are an insect belonging to the order Ephemeroptera, which literally means 'lasting a day.' In case you were wondering."

"I wasn't."

"Whatever. Now for the tour."

"I said no tour."

"Look, it's not a *tour* tour, just me pointing stuff out to you. I'm saying, it's either this or the shelves."

He's got a point, so I fall silent, and for the next twenty minutes Terrance points stuff out to me. A place that sells frozen yogurt and T-shirts ("I buy all my shirts from there"), a nail salon ("If you're into that sort of thing"), and the library ("Their science fiction collection is the worst"). I could fit this whole town in my back pocket.

We pass a storefront with newspaper clippings taped to the window.

"*Black Lake Daily*," Terrance says. "Pretty small operation."

It sure is. There are only two desks inside, one of which is occupied by a woman with bright red dreadlocks.

"That's the editor-in-chief. It's just her and a photographer, but she manages to crawl up in everyone's business anyway."

As we come upon two men sitting outside a small restaurant playing checkers, one of them says, "Hey there, Mr. T. Hot enough out here for you?"

"I'm telling you, it's global warming," Terrance replies. The men laugh and wave him off like a haze of gnats. "That's Dexter and Raymond," Terrance tells me as we walk on. "They play checkers every day, no matter the weather. Ray—the one who said hey—his wife, Jane, owns the diner they were sitting in front of. She makes the best meat loaf in the world, and on Wednesdays she does psychic readings."

"Huh?" I say.

"You know, she tells you what the future holds."

"I *know* what a psychic reading is. I just didn't know you could get one with meat loaf."

My mind starts going as fast as Terrance's mouth. Faster. If the lady who owns the diner can tell the future, maybe she can tell me exactly where to find Dad, so I can tell Mom. Then the two of them can come get Tiffany and me and we can leave Black Lake in our rearview.

I'm so busy imagining driving out of Black Lake without so much as a glance back that when Terrance stops and says, "Aw, man, there's trouble ahead. Quick—let's cross the street!" I keep right on walking.

"Hey, Yuck Mouth."

Two girls are sitting on the back of a bus stop bench just ahead, lined up like crows on a fence.

Terrance waves and starts to cross the street, but they're not going for it. "Come over!" they shout. "We want to talk to you."

We walk over to them slowly. They're chomping on gum, their mouths glistening with tinted lip-gloss.

"Gosh, Yuck Mouth, why you wanna act like you don't know folks today?" one of them says.

"Hey," Terrance says dully.

I stand a good yard away from him, doing my best to adhere to Moving Rule Number Two: *Be invisible. Don't do anything to draw attention to yourself.*

"So, Yuck Mouth," says the same girl who called to him the first time. "Pamela and I were just talking about the best way to way to get a boy to like you. And, well, you're a boy, right?"

"Yeah," Terrance mutters.

"Yeah, right," Pamela says, and snickers.

"Be easy, Pam," the girl says, "Yuck Mouth is a boy. Sort of. And, well, my cousin from Florida says the best way to get a boy to like you is to pretend to have all the same interests as him. Is that true?"

"I don't know," Terrance says.

"Maybe I should ask your friend, then." The girl's eyes find me. She looks me over from head to toe. I pat down my frizzy hair, try to smooth the front of my shorts and KNOWLEDGE IS POWER T-shirt, both stained with pine-scented cleaner. Meanwhile, these girls are done up like they rode a parade float to get here. "What's your name?"

I don't answer. Out of the corner of my eye, I see the girl named Pamela stand up. She's almost as tall as Great-Aunt Grace and nearly as scary.

"Jaguar asked you your name. You slow or something?"

"She's *not*," Terrance says. "Cut it out, Pamela. Her

name is Treasure, but she goes by Jeanie." Terrance moves closer to where I'm standing.

"Wow, Yuck Mouth, you stood up for her right quick. Maybe you found yourself more than a friend. Maybe you got yourself a girlfriend," Jaguar says. She looks like her name, all slinky and light-eyed and ready to pounce.

"She's not my—"

"Where'd you find your girlfriend, anyway?"

"She's staying with her great-aunt, Ms.—Ow!" Terrance glares at me, rubbing his ribs where I just elbowed him. These girls already know my name; I don't want them knowing any more than that.

"Looks like your girlfriend's slow *and* feisty," Pamela says, shaking her head and laughing.

"She's not my girlfriend," Terrance says through clamped teeth.

"That's a shame," Jaguar says, "Because she's a weirdo, just like you like."

And just like that, I've gone from invisible, to visible, to weirdo, and the words jump right out of my mouth before I can stop them: "Pretending to like the same things as a boy just to get his attention is completely asinine."

"Ass-i-*what?*" Jaguar jumps up to join Pamela, and together the two of them walk toward me. I've watched enough Westerns with Dad to know that I need to stand my ground, so I do, until Jaguar and Pamela are standing so close I can see each speck of glitter in their eye shadow.

"You cussing at me?" Jaguar says.

"No. *Asinine* means stupid."

"So you're calling her stupid?" Pamela says, leaning in real close.

I'm eye to eye with her clavicle. I step back a few more yards until I'm standing at the edge of the curb. One more step and I'll be out in the street.

"*No.* I'm calling what she *said* stupid."

"Calling what I *said* stupid and calling *me* stupid are the same thing," Jaguar says, and in an instant, she and Pamela close the distance between us.

"Come on, guys, cut it out," Terrance says, coming to stand beside me again.

"Stay out of this, Yuck Mouth," Jaguar snaps.

And it occurs to me now that I'm going to die.

I'm never going to see Mom or Dad or Tiffany again.

I close my eyes, waiting for the first shove. Punch. Kick to the shins. But it never comes, because a woman shouts, "Yoo-hoo, ladies, what's going on over there?"

I blink and there's a woman crossing the street, waving her giant purse in the air with one hand and holding her wig down with the other. I blink again and she's right beside us, still shouting like she's a block away.

"What's going on over here?" she asks again.

"Oh, nothing. Terrance was just introducing us to his girlfriend," Jaguar says.

"Oh, my, my, my, Terrance. You've only just gotten here and already a girlfriend?"

Terrance opens his mouth to speak, thinks better of it, and just shakes his head instead.

"So will I be seeing all of you at Camp Jesus Saves next week?" the woman asks. She beams at us.

Jaguar matches the woman's perma-grin, watt for watt. "Of course, Ms. Eunetta."

Pamela nods, smiling too.

"I'll be there," Terrance mutters.

"Good, good." The woman turns to me, still beaming. "Eunetta Baxter," she says, holding out her hand for me to shake. "The sheriff's wife."

Eunetta Baxter, loud as a construction site and lumpy as two pillows stuffed in one case. She doesn't know it, but she just saved my life. I shake her hand as she says, "And what about you?" She squints at me. "I don't reckon I've seen you around before. Just move here?"

"Jeanie's visiting," Terrance puts in. "She's staying with Ms. — Ow! Would you quit it already?"

Eunetta's smile falters. "Secretive, aren't you? Well, it's nice to meet you, Jeanie. Let me give you a flier."

Eunetta doesn't see Jaguar roll her eyes — she's too busy digging around in her monster of a purse. She pulls out a bunch of papers and hands one to me. It's a flier just like

Dot's, only there's a picture of some pearls in the center and "$300 reward" printed underneath.

"Y'all call me if you hear even a peep, okay?"

We nod. Eunetta looks over at me again. "So, will I see you at camp next week, Jeanie?" She reaches up to adjust her wig.

I chance a look at Jaguar and Pamela, who are still trying to take me apart with their eyes. "Yeah, will we?" Jaguar asks sweetly.

"No," I say. "I have to, um . . . No. You won't."

"Pity," Eunetta says, shaking her head. "I guess I'll be off, then. You kids behave, you hear?"

"Yes, Ms. Baxter," Pamela and Jaguar say in unison, and as Eunetta makes her getaway, so do I, though not fast enough. I can still hear Jaguar when she calls out, "You'd better watch yourself, weirdo!"

I hear Pamela yell out something else, another threat, and when the sound of their laughter fades, I hear Terrance's footsteps behind me. If it weren't for him, those girls never would've noticed me in the first place. I speed up until I'm walking as fast as I can, leaving Terrance in the dust. He doesn't try to catch up.

Twelve

WHEN I get back to Grace's Goodies, Great-Aunt Grace is sitting behind the counter, which is covered in Hershey's Kisses wrappers. A man sits next to her, a man so tall his torso stretches a good few feet above the countertop. He clears his throat when I come in and Great-Aunt Grace looks up from the newspaper in front of her with narrowed black eyes.

"Don't even think about askin' for one," she says with a pointed look at the Kisses.

"I already told you, I don't like candy."

"I'll bet." She notices the piece of paper in my hand. "What's that?"

"Flier from Eunetta Baxter."

"Give it here."

I hand it to her over the counter. Great-Aunt Grace scans it, as the man reads it over her shoulder.

"Broke into the sheriff's house and robbed his wife?

Dang shame when folks don't respect the law. Look at all that money she's offerin' to get those pearls back."

Great-Aunt Grace takes Dot's crumpled flier from her shirt pocket, smoothes it out, and places it on top of Eunetta's. "I'll give a hoot when she goes up to five hundred," she replies. To me she says, "Where'd Terrance wind up?"

"I don't know," I say, and it's true. On the walk back I kept speeding up, Terrance slowed down, and when I turned around at a stoplight, he was nowhere to be seen.

"You didn't run him off, did you?"

"No, Jaguar and Pamela did."

"Jaguar Burroughs?" Great-Aunt Grace makes a sound in the back of her throat, kind of like a growl.

"Be easy, baby," says the man.

Baby? Let me find out Great-Aunt Grace has a boyfriend. I stare at them, open-mouthed, until Great-Aunt Grace says, "Well, what you standin' there gapin' for, girl? Can't you see I'm tryin' to partake in this here periodical?"

She's eyeing me like she wants to squash me beneath her shoe.

"Where's my sister?"

"Skinny thing, talk you under the table?" the man says. "She's in the back, taking a nap."

I watch as he lights a cigarette. Just what the world needs. Another smoker. He sees me staring at him and winks.

"Name is Moon. I reckon this little lady don't deem me important enough for an introduction." Now he winks at Great-Aunt Grace. She rolls her eyes.

"Is Moon your real name? Because it's kind of ridiculous."

"Says the girl named Treasure," Great-Aunt Grace puts in.

"Real name's Roger," says Moon. "But I was a real fat kid growin' up. Had a face like a moon pie." He fills his cheeks up with air and puffs his face out. Tiffany would think he's a riot. I don't crack a smile.

"What you want, girl?" Great-Aunt Grace asks again.

I grab a pack of Sour Patch Kids off the shelf. "These."

"Thought you said you don't like candy."

"They're for Tiffany."

Great-Aunt Grace smirks. I ignore her as I take the five-dollar bill from my pocket and plunk it down on the counter in front of her. She makes a big show of holding it up to the light to make sure it's not counterfeit.

"Can't trust you folks from up north," she says as she makes her way to the register. She takes her time ringing me up, too. "I'm low on singles, so . . ." Her voice trails off as she counts out my change. In coins. I dump the quarters, nickels, dimes, and more than a few pennies in my left pocket and feel my shorts start to slip down on that side.

Great-Aunt Grace waits for me to say something. I

don't. I go behind the counter and into the stockroom, where Tiffany is stretched out on a blanket on the floor, Mr. Teddy Daniels hugged to her chest. I sit down next to her and rip open the pack of Sour Patch Kids. I concentrate on sitting absolutely still so the cool stockroom air can dry my sweaty back. Man, I can't believe Great-Aunt Grace has a boyfriend. I wonder if Terrance knows that, and then I wonder why I'm wondering about Terrance in the first place.

Great-Aunt Grace and Moon keep up a steady flow of conversation out front, their cigarette smoke snaking its way back here, and I realize that Mom never told Great-Aunt Grace about my asthma. Or she told her, and Great-Aunt Grace just doesn't care. I hold my breath and fan the air in front of me. Moon bounces from topic to topic, from the price of gas to the scarcity of his favorite brand of cigarettes to the broken air conditioner in his car.

"Took it over to H&H Auto Service two weeks ago, but the boss man was out. Left Byron's useless behind in charge. Posted up out front, talkin' to some girl. Took him ten minutes just to notice I was waitin'!"

"Should've taken it to Terhune's over in Bracie, then."

"And burn up all that gas gettin' there? No, ma'am. H&H fixed it just fine, but the boss man ought to send Byron's behind packin'." Moon pauses. "You know, I heard the sheriff's all riled up on account of his wife's pearls. He's plannin' on interviewin' suspects and everything."

"Suspects? What suspects he got? That fool couldn't find his own behind with both hands in his back pockets."

Moon clears his throat. "What you gonna do if he comes round tryin' to question you?"

"Me? What reason he got for questionin' me?"

"On account of what you did to Dot's boy all those years ago."

"Please. I did this town a favor. Let me tell you somethin', if the sheriff come knockin' on my door, I'm gonna make him wish he woulda thought twice."

"Aw, come on, baby. You always gotta be extra. If he comes to your house, just talk to him so he'll leave you alone. Let him in to look around if that's what it takes."

"I ain't lettin' him in nowhere."

"There you go again, makin' things harder than—"

"Hello again, Terrance," Great-Aunt Grace says loudly.

"Hi, Ms. Washington. Hi, Moon," says Terrance. "Hey, listen, Ms. Washington, is Jeanie here? I need to talk to her."

"She's in the back."

At the sound of Terrance's footsteps, I lie down on the blanket and shut my eyes. He says my name softly, and I let out a loud snore in reply. He stands over me for a minute before I hear his feet beat a path back the way he came.

"Say what you had to say?" Great-Aunt Grace asks him.

"Nah."

"You can tell her the next time you see her, then."

"About that, um. I forgot to tell you, but I'm not sure how much I'll be able to volunteer while Jeanie's here. I start camp on Monday."

"What camp?"

"Jesus Saves."

"The Mount Holy Baptist camp? Loudmouth Eunetta Baxter still runnin' it?"

Terrance hesitates. "Yes."

"See if she got room for two more. Wait. Never mind. I'll check it out myself."

Terrance leaves as quietly as he came in.

Just when I thought Black Lake couldn't get any worse, Great-Aunt Grace is talking about sending me to church camp with Pamela and Jaguar. I squeeze my eyes shut until they ache. Even the air feels heavy. Tiffany squirms.

"Mommy?" she calls out.

My eyes snap open. I lie still, waiting to see if she will fall back asleep on her own. But she doesn't. She wakes all the way up, rubs her eyes, and looks around.

"Where's Mommy?"

"She's not here, Tiff-Tiff. We're in Virginia, with Great-Aunt Grace. And the cash register," I add quickly, hoping Tiffany will lie back down.

But it doesn't work. First her lip starts to quiver. Then the tears come.

I sit up, grab Mr. Teddy D., and run through his skit as fast as I can before she gets to howling. The skit doesn't work either. Tiffany keeps crying, and now there's noise. Gulping, hiccupping, calling out for Mom. I reach over to put my arm around her, and my pocket jingles.

"I have something for you."

I pull out the change Great-Aunt Grace gave me.

"You can put it in your Disney Fund when we get back to the house."

Tiffany sniffles and holds out cupped hands. I dump the change in them and she pours it out on the blanket in front of us. We count it together, and for now, it is enough.

Thirteen

OVER the next two days, rumors about a possible suspect have been making their way around Black Lake, and the local paper, *Black Lake Daily,* has a story about it.

"Nonsense." Great-Aunt Grace tosses the paper on the kitchen counter and slams a plate each of burnt waffles and bacon in front of Tiffany and me. She barks, "Tiffany, feed Mr. Shuffle," and leaves the room.

Tiffany groans and gets to her feet. When I hear Great-Aunt Grace's footsteps on the stairs, I get up from my breakfast and pick up the newspaper. Dot's on the front page, cheesing mighty hard for someone who has lost a treasure.

"It says everyone wants to do whatever it takes to put an end to the robberies. The whole town is on edge." I read the article aloud to Tiffany, who is too busy measuring out half a cup of dry food for Mr. Shuffle to listen to me. As soon as he hears the sound of the food hitting his dish, Mr. Shuffle darts in from the living room.

"Crazy old Gag won't even talk to the sheriff," I say, putting the paper back down. "If he comes to interview her, she said she's not going to let him in."

"Do you think Great-Aunt Grace stole those people's stuff?" Tiffany asks, as she peels back the lid on a can of wet cat food.

"She gets out of breath just going up the stairs."

"So? Ow!" Mr. Shuffle swats at Tiffany's ankles. Scowling, she dumps the wet food into his dish and plops it down in front of him.

"So how the heck could she break into someone's house? Still . . ."

"She does have all those figurines . . ."

Our eyes lock. Without another word, the two of us go tearing into the living room. I switch on the overhead light and we take a good long look at Great-Aunt Grace's figurines.

"She doesn't have any elephants," Tiffany says.

"But Moon said the sheriff is probably going to want to speak to her because she stole from Dot's son back in the day." The sheriff probably carries a pistol. No, a shotgun. I gulp. "We need a contingency plan."

"What?"

"Evasive tactics."

"What?"

"A plan of action in case something goes down. This could get ugly."

~~~~~~

Tiffany and I come up with a plan that day, just in case, but the sheriff doesn't make it to Great-Aunt Grace's house until the next night. We are just finishing up a dinner of pork chops and lima beans swimming in too much butter and black pepper when there is a pounding on Great-Aunt Grace's front door. I jump. So does Tiffany.

"Is that them?" she whispers.

Great-Aunt Grace ignores the question and spoons more lima beans onto our plates, even though we've barely touched our first helpings.

"These butter beans are good for you," she tells us. "You'll thank me when you live to be older than me."

We stare up at her blankly. There's more pounding on the front door.

"Aren't you going to get that?" I ask nervously.

"Reckon I should," Great-Aunt Grace replies. "Treasure, when y'all are finished eatin', clear this table and get those dishes washed."

Not a chance. The minute Great-Aunt Grace disappears into the living room, I take Tiffany by the hand, and together we run upstairs to our room, leaving two heaping servings of lima beans and an uncleared table. We shut the door tight behind us. Then we take cover on the floor, just in case the sheriff is out there and he decides to start shooting. Minutes pass.

"We have to stay here until the coast is clear," I say.

"Right," Tiffany says. She raises her head and looks at me. I look at her. We are on our feet and at the window in an instant. I raise the sash as quietly as I can. Crouched on our knees, we peek down at the scene unfolding in front of Great-Aunt Grace's house. There are at least five people standing on the edge of her lawn, one of them a man in uniform. For a while we don't hear anything more than murmuring. Then shouting from the porch.

"Sheriff, y'all got a lot of nerve comin' round my house with this foolishness!"

"It's like I said, Ms. Washington, we just want to talk with you a little, have a look around."

"Go on and look, then."

"Come on, Percy," the sheriff calls from the porch.

The uniformed man at the edge of the lawn takes a step toward the house.

"Y'all can look right from where y'all standin'," Great-Aunt Grace adds, stopping the man in his tracks.

The sheriff comes down off the porch, shouting. "Don't you have any respect for the law?" He's lion-like in size and appearance, a gun holstered at his hip. He's the kind of man most people wouldn't mess with. I'm learning that Great-Aunt Grace is not most people.

"This is the behavior of someone who's got something to hide," Dot shouts. "Mark my words, she stole each and every missing item herself!"

No one says anything. And in this silence Great-Aunt Grace suddenly bursts out laughing. I've never heard her laugh before.

"You're outnumbered, Grace," Dot yells. "We've got your back, Sheriff Baxter. Why don't we just storm the place?"

"I wish you would try stormin' my house, Dot, I really wish you would," Great-Aunt Grace says. As she moves down the porch steps, a car stops down the road and a man and a woman jump out. They hurry toward the scene, stopping a good few yards away. The woman is carrying a notebook and the man a camera.

Great-Aunt Grace walks to the edge of the lawn, stopping a few feet away from Dot and Sheriff Baxter. "Go on and come across my property line, Dot. I dare you. Y'all wanna search my house, you come back with a warrant, you hear?" With each word, she gets closer to them. "Until then, you cross this line and I'll give you what for. Sheriff, you ain't the only one who's packin'. I got a Winchester myself, and Lord knows I never miss."

"She's crazy," I whisper. Tiffany, unable to take her eyes off of the scene playing out before us, just nods.

"As long as we're here, we can't let anyone else know that we're related to her," I tell her. "Do you understand?"

Tiffany's mouth is hanging open; Mr. Teddy Daniels lies abandoned by her side. As if in a trance, she stands up slowly to get a better look.

"Get down!" I jump up to grab her, just as there's a flash and then another.

"What was—"

The woman with the notepad and the man with the camera take off running. I catch sight of the woman's bright red dreadlocks.

"Who was that?" Tiffany asks.

"Editor-in-chief of the local paper and her photographer. They got pictures and everything."

With luck, they didn't catch Tiffany and me in any of their shots. We were all the way upstairs in the window, after all.

~~~~~

But Saturday morning dawns bright and sunny, and Great-Aunt Grace is standing at the kitchen counter, a newspaper spread out in front of her.

"We made the front page," she says.

Bacon is sizzling on the stove, but I'm not even close to hungry anymore. "We?" I ask weakly.

Great-Aunt Grace holds the paper out for me to take it. I do, and there we are, Great-Aunt Grace on her front lawn, arms waving, and me and Tiffany, clear as day, standing in the window for all the world to see.

Fourteen

I wait until the house is dark and Tiffany and Great-Aunt Grace are sleeping before I get up and tiptoe downstairs. Great-Aunt Grace has one telephone, and it's in the living room. I turn on the overhead lights, and there it is, in the far corner beside a stack of old magazines. And there is Mr. Shuffle, curled up on the end of the couch. He looks at me. I look at him. He has paws the size of baby fists.

"Shoo!" I pinwheel my arms around like a maniac, trying to scare him off, but Mr. Shuffle stays right where he is. "Fine."

I crouch on the floor and take the phone off the hook. Mr. Shuffle watches my every move, as I dial Mom's cell phone number, sit back on my heels, and wait. It rings six times before she picks up.

"Hello?" Her voice is thick with sleep.

"Mom? It's Jeanie."

"Jeanie? Treasure—" There's the sound of shuffling,

and I imagine Mom bolting upright to look at the clock. "It's after midnight. Is something wrong?"

"Everything." And for the next few minutes, I tell Mom all about how Great-Aunt Grace is a nut job and that a good number of people believe she's been breaking into houses and stealing valuables and that the sheriff came after her with a gun.

Mom laughs. "Grace is too old to break into anywhere. You don't believe that nonsense, do you?"

"That's not the point. She put our lives in imminent danger."

"You know how many summers I spent with Grace when I was a kid?" Mom says. "And I'm still here to talk about it."

"Well, I'm also feeling a bit wheezy. Her house is like the inside of a vacuum cleaner bag."

"You sound fine to me," Mom says.

"I'm breathing okay *now*, but just you wait. Great-Aunt Grace made us work since the day we got here. Hard. But none of that compares to the gun. When are you coming to get us?"

"I don't know, Treasure."

"Jeanie."

Mom sighs. "I've only just begun looking, *Jeanie*."

"Maybe Dad called our apartment or wrote to us there. Can't you call Mr. Brown and ask?"

"Mr. Brown isn't going to do anything for us, especially

since I didn't send him all the money for the back rent. Look, finding Dad is going to take time."

"How much time?"

"For God's sake, Jeanie, it's only been a few days! You have to be patient."

"*How* patient?"

A long pause. I can almost hear her rubbing that spot between her eyebrows.

"Like a few more days patient?" I go on. "Or a few more weeks? I don't want to stay here anymore."

"I don't know. Probably a week. Maybe two. I just don't know, Jeanie." Mom pauses. "Listen, kiddo, it's late. What do you say the two of us get back to bed? Things won't look so bleak when the sun comes up."

"But—"

"Bed, Jeanie. Now."

"Fine."

I hang up without saying goodbye. Then I stare at Great-Aunt Grace's table, wishing for firm answers instead of halting *maybes* and *probablys*. *Your mother will find your father in exactly two days; you will leave Black Lake in exactly one week, and on this exact date, you will move into a home for good.* I wish I had a crystal ball so I could see what my future holds.

And that's when I remember. The psychic at the diner who does readings on Wednesdays. If Jane can tell the future, maybe she can answer my questions.

Where is Dad?
When will Mom find him?
When will the two of them come for us?
Will we have a home?
I count the days until Wednesday.

Fifteen

R̶ISE and shine! Time to spend a little quality time with the Lord!"

I roll over to squint at the clock. It's 7:30 in the morning. On Sunday, the day of rest. I don't know what's brighter, the light stabbing at my pupils or Great-Aunt Grace standing in the doorway dressed from head to toe in white. White dress, white shoes, white stockings.

"Come on, up, up, up. Service starts at ten, but I like to be a solid forty-five minutes early."

Her church shoes squeak as she comes over to my bed and pulls the covers back. She does the same to Tiffany.

"Got to find you two something decent to put on. You won't shame me on the holy day with your shorts and T-shirts, looking like who thought it and why. Treasure, don't you pull those covers back up!"

I fling them to the side with a groan and slide out of bed like I'm melting as Great-Aunt Grace throws open the dresser drawers and gets to looking. I make my way down the hallway to the bathroom. Tiffany follows, Mr. Teddy Daniels tucked under her arm. I catch a glimpse of our reflections in the mirror. I've been doing the best I can with our hair, especially mine, which is long and tightly curled on the best day, a tangled explosion on the worst. Today is one of the worst. I work on both of us with a brush, some water, and hair bands. I'm wiping Tiffany's face with a damp washcloth when she says, "Should I bring Mr. Teddy Daniels to church?"

I yawn. "He doesn't have any dress-up clothes."

Tiffany's face falls.

"Church is boring anyway," I say quickly. "Let Mr. Teddy D. sit this one out."

When we get back to the room, Great-Aunt Grace has our outfits laid out on our beds.

"Is that your picture-day dress from last year?" Tiffany wants to know. "With the ruffles at the neck?"

It is. I've been pulling clothes out of the chest of drawers for days now and didn't even notice it was in there. Mom must have had the sense to tuck it deep down under.

"Isn't there another dress?" I try to look around Great-Aunt Grace and into an open drawer.

She crosses her arms over her chest and blocks my view. "You mean that dungaree jumper? Not a chance. The Lord's office is not business casual." She peers over my shoulder and into the open closet, where Tiffany and I have piled our dirty clothes from the last few days. "Looks like y'all gonna add a load of laundry to your chores today too."

We stare at her.

"Don't tell me y'all ain't never done laundry, either."

"Mommy did it for us," Tiffany says.

Great-Aunt Grace throws up her hands. "Never met two more spoiled kids in my whole life. Bring them clothes down to the kitchen with you—I'll show y'all how washin' is done."

Just when I thought the day couldn't get any better.

Great-Aunt Grace turns on the heels of her white church shoes and goes marching down the hall. I pull my picture-day dress on, and the first and last time I wore it comes flooding back to me. Picture day at a school in a small Delaware town with only one other black kid. We stayed for three months, and when the teacher announced I was leaving, one of the kids asked if I was going back to Africa.

"I didn't know God had an office," Tiffany says to me as we head downstairs, arms loaded down with dirty clothes. "Do you think the world is his waiting room?"

Sometimes I think Tiffany is the smartest person I know.

Great-Aunt Grace is ready for us downstairs. She's pulled open the big closet adjacent to her back door, exposing her ancient washer and dryer. She starts barking orders at us immediately about water temperature and how much detergent to add. "Half a cup won't get the stink out, girl," she snaps at Tiffany, who snaps back, "We don't stink."

By the time we've got our colored load in and washing, I've worked up an appetite. Trouble is breakfast, like my picture-day dress, hasn't gotten a stitch better with time. We sit down to more too-cooked and undercooked bacon, scrambled eggs with cheese, and home fries. The eggs aren't so bad—just a little dry—but the home fries. Man. Great-Aunt Grace has somehow managed to burn these suckers so bad they look like chips of concrete.

"Do you have any ketchup?"

Great-Aunt Grace takes a bottle from the refrigerator. Nothing quite like cold ketchup on burnt-up, piping-hot food. I wash it all down with a glass and a half of orange juice. When Great-Aunt Grace goes to put the carton of OJ back, I notice that she's got the newspaper article stuck on the front of her fridge with a magnet.

"Y'all are local celebrities now," Great-Aunt Grace says. "Just don't expect anyone to ask you for your autograph."

What I'm expecting is hot stares and glares from people who probably read yesterday's paper and know that we're staying with crazy Great-Aunt Grace. They probably hate us by association.

"We can't go. I'm sick," I blurt out.

"The Lord heals," Great-Aunt Grace replies.

"I can't breathe."

"You can whine, you can breathe, girl. Now, let's go."

I drag myself out of my chair, and Tiffany and I follow Great-Aunt Grace outside. Just when I thought things couldn't get any worse, I realize we have to walk there, and my Mary Janes are already pinching something serious. Since it's Sunday, I phone in a favor to God: *Please save us.*

We make it to the middle of Great-Aunt Grace's road, and Moon pulls up beside us in a long car the color of a pickle and just as lumpy, his windows down and the oldies blaring. Great-Aunt Grace pretends not to see him. Instead, she's got her eyes on Dot, who's on her way to the car parked in her driveway. She's wearing her Sunday best: a full magenta suit and a hat big enough to land a helicopter on. She glares at Great-Aunt Grace, who glares right back and says, "Mornin', Dot, you old fool." If this were a cartoon, steam would be coming out of Dot's ears. Great-Aunt Grace walks on. Tiffany and I follow, Moon still coasting beside the three of us and Great-Aunt Grace still pretending not to see him.

"Aw, come on, Gracie. I told you I was busy," he calls out to her.

She doesn't stop walking. "Busy doin' what? Hidin' while I took on half the town?"

"I wasn't hidin'!" Moon says, indignant.

"You sure enough were." Great-Aunt Grace stops walking and stares at him, sweat beading on her brow. "You's a coward, Moon, simple as that, but I reckon I'll let you drive us anyway."

Moon jumps out to open the passenger-side door for Great-Aunt Grace, and we slide into the back seat. She doesn't thank him, nor does she say a word to him as we drive. Every now and again, he shoots her a nervous look. At last he heaves a great sigh and says, "All right, I should've come by when I heard the sheriff and 'em were on their way to your house. I'm a coward. Happy now?"

"I reckon so," Great-Aunt Grace replies. Moon breathes another sigh, this one of relief, and launches right into his all-time favorite topics: the scarcity of his favorite brand of cigarettes, the price of gas, and lazy Byron, who should be fired from H&H Auto Service.

"I'm telling you, Gracie baby, I drove past there yesterday, and instead of workin' like he supposed to, Byron's useless behind got his head poked into the passenger-side window of some girl's car."

"That's Byron for you," Great-Aunt Grace replies.

"It sure is," Moon says, making a sharp left. "He's a sorry sight. But what's worse is the stores that sell my smokes is dropping like flies. Can't even get 'em up at Sammy's no more. And I'm gonna have to put this car to rest and start hot-stepping it with you pretty soon. Thanks to this war with the Islamists, gas costs as much as diamonds these days. Now, don't get me wrong. I ain't one of them lefties, no, ma'am. My great-grandfather's father fought for his freedom in the Civil War, my daddy fought in World War One, and I faced off against Charlie over in Vietnam. And now look at me, spending half my social security check on gasoline!"

Is hot air the same as gas? Either way, Moon is full of it. I hum along with the oldies on the radio to drown him out.

Soon we pull up to Mount Holy Baptist Church. It's a huge white house with stained-glass windows and columns, smack in the middle of a great big lawn with a parking lot on one side. Moon makes a left into the lot and parks in a spot a few yards away from a side door. He gets out to open Great-Aunt Grace's door. Tiffany and I scramble out, and that's when I notice that Moon is wearing shorts and a T-shirt.

"I don't know how the Lord is going to feel about your outfit," I tell him, shaking my head.

Great-Aunt Grace gives him a hard once-over and says, none too happily, "Moon can't seem to make the time for church."

Moon takes Great-Aunt Grace's hand and kisses it. As he does so, he winks at me.

"So you just drive her here?" I ask, jerking my finger at Great-Aunt Grace.

"Yes indeedy. Every Sunday. Pick her up, too. Come back around one thirty?" he asks.

Great-Aunt Grace frowns. "Better make it two."

I almost choke on my own spit. "Do you mean to tell me church is *four hours?*"

Great-Aunt Grace looks at me. She's wearing makeup. Deep brown foundation that hardly matches her skin, and some kind of burgundy lipstick and blush. I bet she calls the blush "rouge."

"Do you know how long Jesus was up on that cross?" she asks me.

I shake my head.

"A heck of a lot longer than four hours. Now, tuck in your lips and let's go."

Tiffany looks up at me as we follow Great-Aunt Grace toward the door.

"We're going to die in there," Tiffany says mournfully.

I nod. Because it's true.

Sixteen

EVERY eye is on us as we cross the lawn and head toward the church. Conversations come to a halt as we approach people and pick up again in whispers when we pass.

Great-Aunt Grace seems completely unfazed by all this. In fact, she seems to come alive under the weight of this gossip. When she hears someone mention her face-off with the sheriff, she dives in headfirst to talk about how some folks are nothing but a bunch of fools.

"Dot wanted him to break into my house to search it," Great-Aunt Grace says to two women. "Nothin' but wrongdoers themselves, Lord knows."

"Sounds like you got somethin' to hide," says one of the women, fanning herself.

"Ain't no one searchin' my house without a warrant, Barbara, and if folks wanna try, I got somethin' for them that they ain't liable to forget."

Great-Aunt Grace moves on. I reach up and smooth my un-smoothable hair and keep my eyes on my too-tight Mary Janes. I don't know a word to describe the insanity of the woman Mom left us with.

We enter the church. Great-Aunt Grace stops just inside the door and scans the room before turning to us.

"Now, this is how it's gonna be. I'm an usher, so I'll be seatin' folks, and when I'm done, I'll be sittin' up front. You two will be sittin' up there at the end of the last pew, right where I can see you." She points at a balcony, jutting like a cliff over a sea of red carpet and deep brown pews.

"Wait. They let you be an usher?" I ask.

"Who's gonna tell me no?"

Probably no one. Ever. I take Tiffany by the hand and start up the stairs to our seats.

"People are staring at us," Tiffany says.

"Don't stare back."

I try to follow my own advice, but I can't stop checking them out. Most people look at us and then quickly away. One woman whispers audibly to the man beside her, "I didn't even know that crazy old woman had family. Poor things."

With Tiffany at my heels, I hurry to our pew and all but collapse into it. It was hardly a long walk, but I'm sweaty and out of breath all the same. I pull my inhaler out of my dress pocket and take a puff. Then I close my eyes and imagine I'm someplace else. Flying down the highway with Mom in the Explorer, getting closer and closer to Dad. But when I open my eyes again, I'm still in Mount Holy Baptist and the church is starting to fill up. People are milling around, talking, their voices drifting up to the church's high, painted ceiling.

Two women with hats like skyscrapers sit down in front of us. "I can't see," Tiffany whines.

"It's church, Tiffany, not a concert."

One of the women turns around and smiles at me. The other whispers something in her ear, and just like that, her smile disappears.

"Just deal with it, Tiffany."

I lean back against the hard wood of the pew. I can see Great-Aunt Grace showing people to their seats. She's working the middle aisle, and she's not playing with folks. When a man doesn't want to move down to make room for a couple at the end of his pew, she fixes him with a hot stare. He scoots down so fast, it's a wonder he doesn't leave skid marks.

A tall girl walks slowly down the aisle, her arm wrapped tightly around a small, stooped person wrapped in a shawl or a blanket. I watch as the girl helps the figure into a seat. One by one, she removes the coverings until a woman is revealed, wearing a scarf on her head despite the heat. Just before the girl sits herself down, she looks up into the balcony and our eyes lock. It's Pamela. I find another place to rest my eyes.

I choose the stage, where there's a huge painting of black Jesus, staring down at his clasped mahogany hands. Then, for no reason at all, I look around for Terrance. I spot him almost immediately, sitting beside an old woman. He yawns without covering his mouth, and the woman swats at him with her fan. Must be his grandmother, out to save his science-loving soul. Byron is leaning against the far right wall with his arm draped over a girl who's not Sasha. She's giving him all her attention, and he's not even looking at her. I follow his gaze to a long-haired girl sitting a few yards away. What did Great-Aunt Grace say about him? He's got more women than he has sense.

Soon almost everyone is seated and the church is packed. Dad always says that black folks generate heat, and boy, that's no lie. The temperature inside Mount Holy Baptist has gone up a good twenty degrees.

A few people are still looking for seats. One of them is a woman so big, the ground should quake beneath her feet. But it's not her size that makes me stare as she barrels up the stairs toward us. It's what she's wearing—a huge purple hat and a tight purple mini-dress that clings as much to her ample stomach as it does to her ample bosom. Heads turn as she passes, the women rolling their eyes and the men sneaking looks at her impressive cleavage. She joins the women in the pew in front of us.

"Well?" she says to all the folks who have turned to watch her every move. Their heads snap forward. She sucks her teeth and pulls out a fan.

"Morning," says one of the women with the stupid hats. "Where's Raymond today?"

"Back at the diner, minding my business," the big woman says, and laughs.

"You still, uh, practicing them dark arts at your diner?"

The woman plops one hefty arm on the back of the pew and turns to face the women and their preposterous hats. "There ain't a thing dark about telling the future, Ms. Green," she says, and turns back around.

Telling the future?

"Jane?"

Now the woman turns to look at me with heavily made-up eyes. "That's my name, child," she says. "What you calling it for?"

"I have to ask you something."

She faces front again. "If it's about my dress, I don't tell anyone where I shop. My style is couture and I'd like to keep it that way, thank you very much."

"What? No. Is it true that you can . . ."

I stop and look at Jane. Really look at her. Terrance was wrong. She can't possibly tell the future. Psychics are supposed to wear long swirly clothes and go barefoot, not run around in tight purple dresses and sky-high heels with gold sparkles. They should wear scarves of many colors. And they're supposed to have an aura of mystery about them. With the outfit Jane has on, I'm pretty sure I can see *all* her secrets.

"Well, get on with it before the service starts," Jane snaps. She reaches up to pat hair that's not out of place. Her movements have their own soundtrack: the light, tinny sound of two armfuls of gold bangles clinking against each other. Now *those* a psychic would wear.

"I wanted to ask you about my—" I look over at the other two women to make sure they're not listening. They're not. They're too busy talking behind their hands and shooting dirty looks at Jane. Tiffany watches them, fascinated. "I wanted to ask you about my future," I blurt out.

Jane doesn't turn around, but her back stiffens. "You staying with Ms. Washington, ain't you? My neighbor, Lucinda, had her favorite bracelet stolen two weeks back."

"I don't know anything about all this stealing stuff. I just got here a few days ago. So will you tell me my future or not?"

"Not here."

"But—"

The church goes quiet. Not even the rustling of a fan or the turning of a Bible page can be heard. Great-Aunt Grace and the rest of the ushers make their way to the bleachers set up on the small stage. A man as wide as he is tall makes his entrance, wearing a brown suit and shoes. His suit is tight at the thighs and upper arms.

"He looks like a turd," Tiffany whispers, and laughs at her own joke until her eyes get watery.

The man steps to the podium. "Before I get started bringing forth the word of the Lord," he says, "Sister Eunetta Baxter would like to remind all of you that if you signed your children up for our annual Jesus Saves summer camp, the first session begins on Monday morning. If you want your child to attend but haven't yet signed up, Sister Baxter said to come and speak to her."

Eunetta is sitting in the front row. She stands up and addresses the congregation. "As Pastor Burroughs says, the Lord always makes room for one more."

What about two? I chance a look at Great-Aunt Grace. Is she still trying to send us to that camp? My eyes find Pamela again. It's like I can't stop myself. And I can't stop myself from looking for Jaguar, too. I see the back of a head of a girl who could be her, sitting in the first pew, and another in the fourth. I'm not sure, but I start sweating all the same.

"Now, let's get down to business. I'd like to welcome you all back to another Sunday at Mount Holy Baptist Church," Pastor Burroughs shouts. "For those of you who couldn't make it, well, the Lord knows who you are."

Laughter rings out. "Amen," says one of the women with the stupid hats in the pew in front of us.

"Now, ladies and gentlemen, you know that we have been victims here in Black Lake. Victims of self-righteousness and greed."

I can't be positive, but I'm pretty sure Pastor Burroughs cast a look in Great-Aunt Grace's direction when he said "self-righteousness."

"Many of us have been robbed."

"Amen!"

"Burglarized!"

"Yes, Lord!"

"Stupefied!"

"That word doesn't really work in this context," I whisper to Tiffany, but like everyone except me, she has her eyes on Pastor Burroughs. Everyone else, that is, but Byron and his girlfriend. He's staring at the floor. She's staring at him.

"Now, ladies and gentlemen, boys and girls of the congregation, we will not be defeated by the plights of our community. No. We will rise above them, in Jesus's name. Amen."

"A-*men*." The stupid-hat woman again. I have a feeling she's going to be saying that a lot today.

"Like Jesus, we will turn the other cheek, but like God, we will strike the thief down."

I find Great-Aunt Grace among the ushers. She watches Pastor Burroughs, her face stone. Pastor Burroughs wipes his forehead with a handkerchief he's pulled from his breast pocket. He's just getting warmed up. I can tell. "We will not falter; we will not cower. Because the Lord stands behind those who stand up in the name of righteousness. Yes, Lord. God-ah has our backs. Can I get an 'Amen'?"

"Amen!"

"I say, can I get a 'Praise the Lord'?"

"Praise the Lord!"

The whole church is alive now. It's like a pep rally, feet stomping, folks standing up and shouting. And the pastor jumping around the stage, stretching God's name to two syllables, screaming loud enough for the heavens to hear. They can't possibly keep this up for four hours. But they do. Two women faint and have to be brought back with fans and ice water.

Tiffany and I have only been to church a handful of times. Dad says he can get his dose of God without being preached at, thank you very much. But the energy at Mount Holy Baptist is nothing short of electric. Both of us are on the edge of our seats. The pastor calls for a song, and everyone stands up. Neither Tiffany nor I know the melody, but we get to our feet and clap along with the rest of the congregation anyway.

The words to the song say something about living your life in God's light. There are too many people for the singing to be in tune, and the choir, full as it is of old ladies, sounds like a bunch of goats. But the song and the clapping and the foot-tapping are enough to make me feel all tingly inside.

Once the singing is over and we take our seats again, the pastor wipes his brow and says, "Let us bow our heads in a final prayer."

All around me, heads go down.

A while back I prayed once — just once. The way you're supposed to. I clasped my hands, got down on my knees, and looked up to the sky. I did all that when Dad left the first time and Mom seemed to lose her mind, mad enough to slam the kitchen cabinets one minute and crying her eyes out the next. I asked God to send Dad back to us right away, and he did. But it was two weeks later. Now it's been months, and I can't sit around waiting for God to pay attention again.

I poke Jane in the back. Her head snaps up.

"I need you to tell me where my father is. Right now. Please."

I'm speaking just lower than a whisper, but the woman next to Jane looks at me and puts her finger to her lips.

Jane shakes her head, her back to me. "I said, not here."

"Please. It's a matter of life and death."

Jane breathes in through her nostrils and then out through her mouth. "Look, it doesn't work like that. I can't tell you where your father is."

"Well, can you look into the future and tell me when he's going to come back so we can be a family again?"

"Psychic predictions cost five dollars."

"I left my money at home."

Jane turns around in her seat and looks at me. "Guess you better join in on this prayer, then."

The woman beside Jane looks about ready to explode. She shushes me again, but I act like I don't notice.

"Please," I say to Jane. "I'll pay you later. I promise."

Jane says nothing.

"I wouldn't lie in church."

Jane considers this. Then she faces front, closes her eyes, and bows her head, looking for all the world like a woman deep in prayer. She turns her head slightly and says quietly to me over her shoulder, "It seems you've spent some time being jerked around by things you can't control. You're unhappy now, but you gotta be willing to make sacrifices. Happiness doesn't come easy, Lord knows that's the truth, but you gotta hang in there and fight for it. And you can't go giving up hope, either. If you do, it's like giving up the will to go on."

The prayer comes to an end, and people raise their heads and slowly begin to stand. One of the women next to Jane clears her throat and with a toss of her head indicates the line of people waiting to file out of the pew. Jane heaves herself up, adjusts her hat and her bosom, and starts for the stairs.

I stop her with my hand on her arm. "What about my father? Is he in my future?"

"Happiness is. Take that for what it's worth."

Jane removes my hand from her arm and goes on her way, leaving me with hope in one hand and happiness in the other.

Seventeen

FOR the rest of the afternoon, Jane's words tumble around my head like they're doing cartwheels, backflips. I feel like I could do the same. Like I could fling my inhaler aside and run three whole miles without stopping. Even cleaning shelves at Grace's Goodies after church can't bring me down.

"Girl, what you grinnin' about?" Moon asks when I go out to the front to find out where Great-Aunt Grace put the pine-scented cleaner. "You been at it since I picked y'all up."

Great-Aunt Grace looks over at me. "Must've been the service. The Lord does work in mysterious ways," she says. "You'd know that if you came to church every once in a while."

Moon's smile slides off his face.

The door swings open and Terrance walks in. I turn on my heels and return to the stockroom and go to the shelf where Great-Aunt Grace told me I could find the cleaner.

Soon Terrance appears in the stockroom too. He stops beside me and starts moving boxes around.

"I thought you weren't coming back while I'm here."

"I thought you were sleeping when I said that." He eyes me. He's wearing a T-shirt with a planet on it, or maybe an atom. "I left my sketchpad here. Have you seen it?"

I shake my head and take the cap off the cleaner. Out of the corner of my eye, I watch Terrance check shelf after shelf until at last he says, "Don't worry, I found it," and pulls his sketchpad from behind a box of Skittles. At that moment Great-Aunt Grace shouts, "Terrance, Treasure, get out here!"

As we hurry to the front, I trip over a huge cardboard box sitting right in the entrance to the stockroom. Terrance trips over me, and together the two of us are sprawled on the floor behind the register, a tangle of arms and legs. Tiffany bursts out laughing.

"Shut up," I snap, but she's too busy laughing herself stupid. I glare at her as Terrance gets to his feet. He holds his hand out to help me, but I get up on my own, rubbing my throbbing knee.

"Why is that box there, trying to kill someone?" I ask Great-Aunt Grace, who's bent at the waist, peering at something on the shelf below the register. I peek over her shoulder. She's working the dials on a safe. She pulls it open, takes out an envelope, and pushes the safe closed. Then she stands and turns to face me.

"What, girl?"

"That box you left right in front of the storage room"—I point down—"almost killed me."

"And me," Terrance adds pointedly.

I ignore him. "What's in it?"

"My security system."

The front of the box reads Ironclad Surveillance and has a picture of a complicated-looking camera on it. I look around for a camera, but I don't see one anywhere. Then I realize that the box hasn't even been opened.

"Y'all gonna stand there and look at it, or y'all gonna move it?" Great-Aunt Grace says.

We're still standing over the box, eyeing it. Terrance uses the toe of his sneaker to nudge the box into a corner.

"Good. Now, Moon and I are runnin' to the bank so I can unload some cash in the depository box," Great-Aunt Grace tells us.

"Are we gonna watch the store?" Tiffany asks eagerly.

"No," Great-Aunt Grace says flatly. "I'm gonna lock the door while I'm gone and put a sign up sayin' I'll be back in twenty minutes. Don't let anybody in, don't eat any of my candy, and if you want to keep your fingers, you won't touch my register."

Terrance pipes up, "But I'm not—"

Great-Aunt Grace turns to go, but not before giving each of us a good hard look. I can hear the keys in the lock a second after the door closes behind her.

"—supposed to be staying," Terrance finishes weakly. He heaves a sigh. "Guess we may as well work on the shelves, since I'm trapped here." Neither of us moves in the direction of the stockroom. I take Great-Aunt Grace's seat in front of the register. Terrance leans against the counter and flips through his sketchbook.

I watch people pass by. There isn't a one of them who doesn't stop and peek into the store. That includes Jaguar and Pamela, who make eye contact with me and take their sweet time moving on.

"What's the deal with those two?" I ask.

Terrance looks up from his sketchpad, just missing them. "What two?"

"Never mind."

Tiffany hops down from her stool and goes over to the shelves of candy. She holds her chin in her hand as she ponders. After careful consideration, she plucks a box of Mike and Ikes off the shelf and returns to her seat.

"Jeanie, pay for these," she says, and rips open the box of candy.

"You can't boss me around," I tell Tiffany. Terrance is doing a pitiful job of trying to hide a smile.

Tiffany pops two Mike and Ikes in her mouth and closes her eyes, to savor the taste or to completely ignore me. I take seventy-five cents from my pocket and place the coins next to the register. Just then there is a knock on the door.

"We're closed!" I shout.

With the glare from the sun, I can see only the outlines of two people. They knock again. And again. I start for the door.

"You're not supposed to open it," Tiffany says to my back.

I unlock the door and open it just a crack. "We're closed."

"Says who?" comes the voice of a girl.

"Uh-oh," Terrance says, but it's too late.

The door is shoved open. I have to jump back to avoid a blow to the face that would have knocked me out cold. Jaguar enters, followed by Pamela, both wearing tiny khaki shorts. Back in Jersey, girls called those shorts "poom-pooms."

"Hey, weirdo," Jaguar says. Pamela says nothing. She stays by the door and keeps glancing into the street.

Jaguar pushes past me and proceeds to size up the goods, stalking around like a lioness on the plain. "Oh, hey, Yuck Mouth," she says to Terrance, as she inspects the rack of candy closest to the register. "Hmmm, what am I in the mood for today?"

"I *said*, we're closed."

Jaguar stops and looks at me. She turns her body first, places her hands on her hips. Her head whips around last. Mom calls this "attitude stance."

"What did you say?" Jaguar asks.

I bring myself up to my full height, which makes me an inch taller than she is.

"Pam, did you hear all that attitude?"

Pamela drags her eyes from the street and comes to stand beside Jaguar. No matter how straight I stand, I'll never be as tall as Pamela. Jaguar walks right up to me until she's standing so close the toes of our sneakers touch. I stare into her flame-colored eyes and then into Pamela's dark, murky ones.

"We didn't hear you. Right, Pam?" Jaguar says. "Would you mind hitting rewind?"

I take a step back. Jaguar steps forward. So does Pamela.

"I said we're closed." I'm stuttering so bad I sound like a CD skipping. "The woman who owns this store went out and said she'd be back in twenty minutes. There's a sign on the door. Ms. Washington left it," I add, in case they fear the wrath of Great-Aunt Grace like anyone with sense should.

Pamela falls back, just a little. But not Jaguar. "Ms. Washington? You mean your kin? Everyone knows you're related to her now, so quit fronting, and everyone thinks she's a big old thief. So there." Jaguar turns and gives her poom-poom-clad butt a smack. "Now, shut up while me and Pam do what we came to do."

I shut up and watch as Jaguar grabs up a huge handful

of candy from one shelf and dumps it on another. She does that over and over again and mixes everything around with her hands, until almost nothing is where it should be. Then she takes a pack of Starburst for herself. At Jaguar's urging, Pamela takes a Hershey bar.

"You could get arrested for this," Terrance says.

"Go on and call the sheriff, Yuck Mouth," Jaguar says. "I'll tell him you three did it, and he'd believe me, too. Him and my daddy been tight for years."

Jaguar glances at Terrance, daring him to call the sheriff. Terrance doesn't move.

"That's what I thought," Jaguar says, and turns to Pamela and her Hershey bar. "That's all you're gonna take?"

Pamela mutters something about having just eaten. Jaguar rolls her eyes. "Whatever," she says. "Watch this."

With a swipe of her arm, Jaguar knocks the contents of one shelf to the floor, then another. Packs of Skittles and M&M's plummet down, followed by Kit Kats and Twix bars.

"You can't do that!" Tiffany shouts, but Jaguar is on a roll. By the time she decides to stop, the floor around her is covered in Great-Aunt Grace's merchandise. After kicking the mess around and stomping it a few times, Jaguar calmly plucks a pack of unscathed sour watermelons off the floor and brings them over to the counter along with her pack of gum.

"I'll take these," she says. "You getting that, Pam?" She points at the Hershey bar Pamela's been holding.

Pamela hardly seems capable of speech. She shakes her head.

"Whatever," Jaguar says, shrugging. She takes out a crumpled dollar bill and tosses it on the counter.

"You're bugging, Jaguar," Terrance says.

"Shut up, Yuck Mouth," Jaguar snaps. "Let's go, Pam."

Before they leave, Pamela puts the chocolate bar back on the shelf where it belongs.

"Be seeing y'all," Jaguar calls sweetly over her shoulder. The door swings shut behind them.

"They won't be seeing *me*," I say.

"Or me," Tiffany puts in.

"They will if Ms. Washington sends you to Camp Jesus Saves tomorrow," says Terrance.

"Wait. Camp?" Tiffany says slowly.

"Yes. Camp. With those two lunatics. I can't believe Jaguar did this," I say.

I go around the counter to inspect the damage. There are packs of candy everywhere. "We'll never get all this back on the shelves before Great-Aunt Grace gets back. She's going to kill us."

"She is," Terrance agrees.

Tiffany says, "I love camp. Remember Camp Dream Lake, Jeanie?"

I remember poison ivy and an asthma attack from a forced hike up the side of a mountain. I bet Jaguar and Pamela will leave me with even worse memories.

"We're not going to camp," I tell Tiffany. "Now, help me clean this place up."

Terrance hurries around the counter to help. While Tiffany stays put on her stool, Terrance and I pick up candy by the handful and all but throw it on the shelves, trying to get it all fixed before Great-Aunt Grace and Moon come back.

No such luck. They push through the door of Grace's Goodies moments later, and the store still looks like someone shook it up and set it back down again.

"What in the sweet name of Jesus happened here?" Moon cries.

Great-Aunt Grace's eyes sweep over the floor and her messed-up shelves. She doesn't say a word.

"Jaguar did this," I say. "She and Pamela forced their way in."

Great-Aunt Grace makes a growling sound in the back of her throat. Moon reaches over and touches her gently on the arm.

"You should call the cops and have Jaguar thrown in jail!" I say.

Great-Aunt Grace's nostrils flare.

"Be easy, baby," Moon says. "Jaguar's just a kid."

Moon must be six and a half feet tall. Great-Aunt Grace looks at him like he's four foot two.

"Jaguar's going to pay for this," she says, and I can tell she means business.

"When?" Tiffany asks eagerly.

"In good time."

"In good time?" I shriek.

Great-Aunt Grace raises her eyebrows at my raised voice.

I clear my throat. "Okay, like you said: in good time. Speaking of time . . ." I figure now is as good as any, so I just blurt it out: "This is why you can't send us to that camp with Jaguar. Bad influences all around. So we're not going."

"Oh, yes, you are."

"We are *not*. If what Jaguar did here isn't proof that Camp Jesus Saves is falling short of its name, I don't know what is."

"You don't worry yourself none about Jaguar. She's gonna get what's coming to her, best be sure of that," Great-Aunt Grace says calmly. "But you goin' to camp, girl, you and your sister. Now you and Terrance get back to them shelves."

"But I'm not—" Terrance says.

"Git," Great-Aunt Grace snaps.

"—staying," Terrance finishes weakly.

We head back into the stockroom, Jane's words

tumbling through my mind again. *Don't give up hope.* I won't, only now I'm hoping for some new stuff. I hope Great-Aunt Grace comes down with amnesia between now and tomorrow morning and forgets all about sending us to Camp Jesus Saves.

Eighteen

WE'VE been in Black Lake for six days, and if I should've learned anything by now, it's that all the hope in the world isn't going to help when it comes to Great-Aunt Grace. I wake up to find her standing over my bed, a glass of orange juice in her hand.

"I'm not going to camp," I tell her.

"Oh, yes, you are. Y'all ain't gonna be nippin' at my ankles all the Lord's day long. Besides, a little Jesus ain't never hurt a soul."

But I bet Jaguar and Pamela could cause someone some real damage.

"I want y'all downstairs in thirty minutes or less. Understood?"

"I guess."

I wait for Great-Aunt Grace to leave. She doesn't. Instead she stops just by the door and points at the clean laundry sitting on top of the dresser. She made Tiffany and me finish it last night. "That's what y'all call foldin'?"

I nod. Great-Aunt Grace disappears into the hallway, muttering about how the Lord never made two more useless kids. I get up to shake Tiffany awake. She swats at me like a cat. I say just one word—"Camp"—and she flies out of bed. She doesn't complain when I scrape her hair into a ponytail or when I get in her ears with a washcloth, or even when she has to feed grumpy old Mr. Shuffle, who goes after her ankles again when she takes too long opening his can of 9 Lives. When Great-Aunt Grace serves us up oatmeal with the consistency of cement, Tiffany doesn't so much as make a face.

Not me. I can barely choke down my breakfast, not even when Great-Aunt Grace comes and stands over me the way she does.

"You gonna be hungry in no time, and you'll have no one to blame but yourself," she says.

For Camp Jesus Saves, I have no one to blame but Great-Aunt Grace.

I take my time washing the breakfast dishes, soaping and rinsing each dish more than once. When she catches me soaping up the sponge to rewash the cups for the fourth time, Great-Aunt Grace says, "You gonna wash the clean right off them dishes, girl. Now, come on and let's go."

To camp. We lock up the house and start walking in the Black Lake heat, and even though I try to walk slower than a tortoise with a bum leg, we're at camp in no time. It's a

scientific fact that the more you don't want to go somewhere, the faster you'll get there. We stop in front of Fannie Lou Hamer Middle School. A banner strung across the
school's brick front shouts in all caps: WELCOME TO CAMP
JESUS SAVES, WHERE DELIVERANCE IS FREE.

We follow Great-Aunt Grace up the walkway and
through the front door. Fannie Lou Hamer Middle School
smells like fried food and permanent markers. Our shoes
squeak on the linoleum floor. Two girls come running
down the hallway, holding hands. When they see Great-
Aunt Grace, they slow to a walk and move all the way to the
right, hugging the wall. "Uh, hi, Ms. Washington," one of
them says. Great-Aunt Grace nods in response and keeps
right on going. She leads us straight down a hallway still
lined with posters and projects from the past school year,
not stopping until we're through another door and back
outside, where there are picnic tables set up with kids
around them.

"Now, where's that loudmouth Eunetta?" Great-Aunt
Grace mutters, looking around.

In the end, Eunetta finds us before we find her. She's
running toward us, holding down her wig with one hand.
She's got a clipboard in the other. She stops a few feet shy
of the three of us, and it takes her more than a moment
to get her breath back. Then she manages to choke out,
"Camp is full."

"Thought the Lord always makes room for one more," Great-Aunt Grace says.

Eunetta's eyes go wide as her own words fly back at her and hit her right in the face.

"He does, of course, but we're just more full up than we thought." Eunetta taps her clipboard for emphasis. "So sorry." She doesn't sound sorry at all.

Great-Aunt Grace points at a spot of shade beneath a tree. "You two, go over there. I need to have a word with Ms. Baxter in private."

For Great-Aunt Grace, private means right where the two of them are standing. Tiffany and I watch from our spot in the shade as Great-Aunt Grace and Eunetta go at it. Eunetta starts waving her clipboard around.

"Why doesn't that lady want us here?" Tiffany asks.

"Because we're related to Great-Aunt Grace." I think of the smile Eunetta fixed me with the first time she met me, when she didn't know that. Now her face is puckered up tight as a fist.

Great-Aunt Grace takes a step closer to Eunetta.

"Oh, my God, she's going to smack her up," I say.

Tiffany and I watch, rapt, waiting for Great-Aunt Grace to lay hands on loudmouth, clipboard-brandishing Eunetta Baxter. The moment never comes. Great-Aunt Grace's hands stay in her pockets as she leans in real close to Eunetta and says something I can't hear. Eunetta throws up her hands and says, "All right! I'll make room for them, but they better not step a toe out of line."

The two of them come over to Tiffany and me. Eunetta stops to write something down on her clipboard.

"You hear that, girls?" she says. "Not. A. Toe. Out. Of. Line."

"You got kids here right now worse than these two, trust me," Great-Aunt Grace says. It's probably the nicest thing she'll ever say about us.

Eunetta purses her lips and flips to a page in her clipboard. Just then, Terrance comes flying out of the building, holding on to his sketchpad. "Ms. Eunetta, we're out of—" He stops dead in his tracks when he sees me. "Oh. Hi."

I give him a halfhearted wave.

"What is it that you need, Terrance?" Eunetta asks impatiently.

"They're out of drawing paper." Terrance is talking to Eunetta, but his eyes are on me. I look off into the distance at a bunch of little kids running around a tree.

"Check with Miss Donna. She said she was going to pick some more up yesterday."

"Okay," Terrance says, and turns to leave.

"Wait," Eunetta says, holding out her free hand. She looks from him to me, remembering. "You two are friends, right?"

I shake my head. Eunetta rolls her eyes.

"Be that as it may, you already know each other and you're in the same group. Terrance, show Treasure to Group Twelve."

"Jeanie," I tell her. "I go by my middle name."

Eunetta crosses something off on her clipboard and frowns. "Tiffany will be in Group Seven. Your name *is* Tiffany, right? They're down there doing arts and crafts. Terrance can walk you—"

There's no need. Tiffany takes off running. I watch as she goes right up to the counselor and introduces herself. She's sitting down at the table in no time, reaching for a paintbrush. That sure enough won't be my MO. After what happened with Jaguar and Pamela, I have to draw as little attention to myself as possible, which means strict adherence to Moving Rules One and Two: *Don't make friends* and *Be invisible.*

"So they're all settled, then?" Great-Aunt Grace says, checking her watch. "I need to get to the store."

"They're as settled as they're gonna be," Eunetta says through clenched teeth.

"Good. Y'all behave yourselves. Some folks are just waitin' for the two of you to slip up." She gives Eunetta a hard look, then shifts her eyes to me. "Come over to Goodies when you're done. Terrance can show you the way." Great-Aunt Grace exits stage left, leaving me with Terrance, Eunetta, and Eunetta's stank attitude.

"Our group is finishing up in arts and crafts," Terrance

says. "We do drawings and murals, not baby stuff." He holds up his sketchpad with a drawing of a very complicated machine with a seat and lots of buttons. "Then we're going to the lake."

He indicates that I should follow him inside, and I do. So does Eunetta. I keep my distance from both of them, but especially Terrance. He stops in front of room 107 and holds the door open for me.

"You go on inside, Terrance. I want to have a word with Jeanie," Eunetta says, smiling.

The door closes behind Terrance, and Eunetta's smile melts right off of her face. "Look, your great-aunt is trouble, and from what I know, trouble tends to run in the blood, so listen to me and listen good: I've got my eyes on you."

Eunetta's eyes are too close to a nose shaped like a greater-than symbol. "Okay," I tell her. "That's cool."

She glares at me. The door swings open and Group Twelve files out, first the counselor—brown-skinned with box braids, probably in high school and definitely too perky—followed by the campers.

"We're off to the lake, Ms. Eunetta, to see one of God's many miraculous works."

Terrance, still holding on to his sketchpad, is in the front of the line. Jaguar and Pamela are last. I fall into step after them because I have to, lagging as much as I can without getting left behind, but that doesn't stop them from whispering and turning around to stare at me the whole way to the lake. Eunetta is not the only one with her eyes on me. May as well change this place's name to Camp Kill Me Now.

Nineteen

IT never occurred to me that Black Lake got its name from an actual lake, but our counselor—whose name happens to be Sunny—leads us through a small park five minutes from Fannie Lou Hamer Middle School, across a stretch of grass, and toward a mass of tall trees. There's a narrow dirt trail between them. Their big, barrel-shaped trunks make them look like they're standing guard, protecting something sacred. Or forbidden.

Is it safe in there? I wonder, but I don't ask.

I hang back, maintaining a safe distance from Jaguar and Pamela, thinking about bears and cougars with claws and teeth like steak knives. But everyone else is walking along, seemingly not in fear of being snatched and mangled. I stumble over a tree root and almost fall.

"Walk much?" Jaguar asks, and laughs herself stupid.

Now I'm really hoping for a cougar or a bear or, at the very least, a psychotic chipmunk to nip at her ankles. With this comforting image nestled in my mind, I look around. It is beautiful in here. The way the sunlight trickles down between the branches and sits in golden puddles on the ground, the smell of pine. Not sharp and stinging like the cleaner I have to use at Grace's Goodies, but soft and cool like baby powder.

When we come to an opening between the trees, I'm kind of disappointed to leave the woods behind. "Kind of" turns into full-on disappointment when I get my first glimpse of the lake. The water is surrounded by dingy sand and closed in by trees on all sides. It might qualify as a river. No, too small. More like a pond. The dark water is coated with green scum and writhes like something alive.

"Welcome to Black Lake," Sunny declares, our official tour guide. She gestures to us to move in closer. The line dissolves as we cluster around her. I make sure to stand as far away from Jaguar and Pamela as possible.

"What's the first thing that comes to your mind when you look at it?" Sunny scans the faces of Group Twelve, and her eyes stop on me. Of course. She beams. "This is your first time seeing Black Lake, isn't it?"

A dozen heads swivel around to look at me. Some kids lean in at first and then rock back on their heels.

"That's that girl from the paper, the one who was all up in Ms. Washington's window when she disrespected the sheriff?" someone says.

"Yeah, that's her. They're related or something. You saw them leaving church yesterday, right, Pam?" Jaguar again.

I swallow hard. I open my mouth, then close it, like a dying fish. In the end, it is Sunny who yanks me off the hook.

"Think about it and you can share later if you want to." She turns her attention to the entire group again. "What we want to focus on today is the beauty of the natural world, bestowed upon us by our Almighty Father."

"It's man-made," someone whispers behind me. It's Terrance, and for the next few minutes as Sunny waxes on about Black Lake being an example of the beauty of God's natural world, Terrance tells me in a low voice that it was hardly a miracle, but a result of Black Lake being land-locked. "They wanted a body of water," he says, "so they made one. Plain and simple."

Sunny is still rhapsodizing poetic on Black Lake, but fewer than half the kids are listening. "Let's use the next fifteen minutes to walk around and take it all in," she says.

"It's gross," one kid says, pointing at the green scum on the lake's surface.

"What is that gunk floating right there?" another asks.

"It's algae." Terrance. Everyone except Sunny and me looks at him like he has two heads. "You asked, John," he says. "I answered."

"Fuh-reak," Jaguar says. Laughter rings out all around. Terrance just shakes his head.

The Twelves split up to explore, most of them going right. I go left, walking the length of the shore until I find a big, bumpy rock. I toss it from hand to hand, cock back, and throw it with all my might into the lake. It makes a small splash.

"That's not how you skip rocks," says Terrance, coming up behind me. "Find a flat one, and flick your wrist." Terrance sets his sketchpad down gingerly on a dry spot in the sand and goes in search of a stone. He's back moments later. "This one'll do. Flat ones are the best for skipping. Okay. Ready?" I don't nod or say yes, but Terrance walks me through his rock-skipping lesson anyway. He takes it all quite seriously, and since I don't have anything else better to do, I scan the ground for flat stones. When I find a few, I slip all but one into my pocket. Then I do exactly what Terrance told me to. I flick my wrist and send the first stone soaring, like I'm trying out for the stone-skipping Olympics. It skips three times.

Terrance pumps his fist in the air. "Now, *that's* what I'm talking about! If you believe what my cousin says, two skips means two wishes."

"What?"

"It's this game she used to play with her friends called skipping wishes. For every skip you get a wish." Terrance pauses. "So you gonna wish or what?"

"Wishes don't come true if you say them aloud. Everybody knows that."

"I'll leave you to it, then," Terrance says.

I close my eyes and wish for Mom to find Dad and for the next place we live to be our last place. The perfect place. I skip a bunch more rocks. By the time I notice Pamela standing a few feet away, staring, I've wished for a trip to Disney World for Tiffany, a pair of sky-blue Converse for me, and at least one decent meal while we're at Great-Aunt Grace's house, because there are some things you can't wish for enough.

"What are you doing?" Pamela asks. Instinctively I look around for Jaguar. She's farther down the shore, talking to John and another boy.

"Are you just, like, throwing rocks?" Pamela says. Her tone tells me that no matter what I say I'm doing—skipping stones or walking on water—she's going to say it's stupid. But she asked, so I answer in as few words as possible.

"Skipping wishes."

"What's that?"

"Skip a stone. Number of times it skips is how many wishes you get."

"Wishes, huh?" Pamela picks up the stone nearest her foot. She attempts to do something with it that in no way resembles skipping.

"Terrance could show you how to do it," I say.

I catch Terrance's eye. He mouths, "No way."

"I can do it on my own," Pamela says.

I shrug and turn my back to her. I hear one stone after another belly-flop into the water until Pamela hurls her last one in with so much force, it arcs high in the air like a comet before plummeting back down. "This is stupid," she says, and storms off to join Jaguar.

"What's her problem?" Terrance says, joining me at the water's edge.

"What isn't?"

"I found some more good rocks to skip. Here, you can have some."

I hold out my cupped hands, and that's when Jaguar and Pamela start blowing loud, sloppy kissy noises at Terrance and me. I jerk my hands back so fast the rocks fall to the ground. Most of them land on Terrance's feet.

"Ow! What's *your* problem?"

"You attract too much negative attention, and I don't need any more of that."

I move farther along until I come to a curve in the shore. I can't see Terrance's face from here, but I can still hear Jaguar and Pamela and their stupid kissy noises.

Twenty

WHEN we get back to Camp Jesus Saves, it is time for lunch. I take my turkey and cheese sandwich and juice box and find just the right table to guarantee I'll be left alone: the one mostly in the sun and right next to a row of garbage cans. But of course, just as I'm removing my crusts, Terrance walks over with his backpack and his tray and sits down across from me and two seats away.

"I don't know where you're from, but where I'm from they consider this stalking."

He holds up his hand, palm out. "I'm in your orbit, but not in your space."

What? The word almost escapes, but I hold it prisoner. I've talked to Terrance too much today. It's time for me be stricter about Moving Rule Number Two and get serious about being invisible. Maybe then he'll get the point.

He reaches into his pockets and pulls out a wrinkled piece of drawing paper and a nubby pencil. Everything about him seems wrinkled, as if he had been crumpled up in someone's fist. He tries unsuccessfully to smooth the paper out with both hands.

"I used to have a folder for my collection of sketches, but I lost it and all the work inside it," he says, as if I care. "I don't want to start over, though, because it's never the same when you do. You know what I mean?"

I've been moving for as long as I can remember, and each time, Dad said we were starting over. I look down at my tray, willing myself not to answer.

"So we're doing the silent thing again? That's cool."

Terrance turns his attention to his paper and his sandwich, so engrossed in the two of them he seems to forget about me. I chance a peek, and he looks up and catches me. Of course.

"It's a homemade lightning rod," he explains. "Trying to detect thunderstorms before they start. It's not a complicated design—it's more . . ." Terrance gropes around for a word.

"Rudimentary?" The word escapes before I can stop it.

If Terrance is surprised that I spoke, he doesn't show it. "What does that mean?"

"Limited to the basics. Simple."

"Like Jaguar's brain?"

"Exactly."

Terrance reaches into his backpack and pulls out another piece of paper, this one more wrinkled than the first. He rips it in half. "Will you write it down for me? That word and what it means?" He places his pencil on the paper and slides it over to me.

I write down *rudimentary* and its definition, along with the words *Hint: Jaguar's brain.* And then, as if she knows we are talking mess about her, Jaguar is there, standing behind Terrance's chair, along with her faithful sidekick, Pamela.

"Are y'all exchanging phone numbers, Yuck Mouth?" Jaguar asks, slapping Terrance on the back.

"No," he says.

"Then what's on the paper?"

"Nothing."

Jaguar comes around the table to get a better look. I try to snatch the paper, but she is as quick as her namesake. She reads it aloud, stumbling on *rudimentary*. Maybe she won't get it.

"Who wrote this?" she demands in a voice like battery acid.

She gets it.

Before I can own up to it, Terrance says, "I did."

Jaguar balls up the paper and throws it at him. It bounces off his forehead and lands in his lunch. And, for good measure, she picks up the untouched half of his sandwich and finishes it off in four greedy bites.

"You keep it up, Yuck Mouth, and you and your girl-friend are gonna be sorry," Pamela says without much conviction. They saunter off, but not before Jaguar helps herself to Terrance's juice box.

"Okay, I see what you mean about attracting negative attention," he says when Jaguar and Pamela are out of earshot.

"Why do you let those girls pick on you like that?"

"They pick on everybody. Besides, where I'm from, men don't get loud with women." Terrance sits up a little straighter and puffs out his chest. I try not to laugh.

"And where's that again?"

"Mississippi. What about you?"

"Recently? New Jersey, Delaware, Pennsylvania, New York State."

"Huh? Your father in the military or something?"

"Here, take half of my sandwich." It's the least I can do, considering he lost his lunch lying for me.

"Thanks."

We eat in silence for a few moments before Terrance licks mayonnaise from the corners of his mouth and tries again. "So, where are your parents?"

"Where're your friends?"

Terrance reels back, as if I've hit him. I look away and come up with Moving Rule Number Three: *Don't feel.*

"Look," I say. "I'm sorry. But it's not like I haven't been sending out signals since I got here. I'm not looking for friendship."

Terrance looks down at the picnic table. It's not much to look at, and yet he seems to be studying it, his nose barely an inch from the surface. He points. "Carpenter bees."

"What?"

"Look around at all the holes in this table."

"It's an old table." Everything in Black Lake is old, and bees have nothing to do with it.

"Those kind of holes aren't from age. Carpenter bees made them. They carve out nests in wood. If you're not careful and you stick your finger in one of these holes, the female bee is likely to sting you good." Terrance closes one eye and peers into the hole nearest him with the other. "Kids around here don't get me," he says.

"And you think *I* will?"

"I guess. I mean, you have that shirt, the one that says KNOWLEDGE IS POWER, and you weren't even wearing it like, I don't know—"

"Ironically?"

"What does that mean?"

"It means I don't wear that T-shirt to make fun of people who believe knowledge is power. I really do think it is."

"I agree." Terrance looks up at me. "See? Maybe I kind of get you, too." He studies my face like he studied the holes in our picnic table. Then he takes out yet another wrinkled sheet of paper from his backpack, rips a tiny piece from it, and hands it to me. "Can you write down what *ironically* means for me too? Or maybe you can do it tomorrow. At lunch?"

He's asking to sit with me again. He isn't so bad, so long as he doesn't talk about his tarantula or ask questions about Mom and Dad or—

Remember the Moving Rules.

"Okay, but we're not friends."

"What are we, then?"

Dad knew guys at work when we were in Cedar Hills. Sometimes he'd meet up with them for a drink; he even had them over for a card game once. He didn't introduce us to them, though, and he never said he'd miss them when we left. He had a special name for them.

"We're associates," I tell Terrance.

"Associates," he says slowly, rolling the word around in his mouth as if he's trying to get a taste for it. "Okay." He holds out his hand. "Shake on it?"

We shake on it.

In the distance, someone blows a whistle, signaling the end of lunch. Terrance stands up and shoves his papers in his backpack, including the crumpled definition of *rudimentary.* He slips his pack on. "I think we have Bible study next."

"Seriously?"

"Yeah. Ms. Eunetta runs it."

"That's weird."

"What is?"

"I'm awake and yet I'm still having a nightmare."

Terrance laughs. This is the first time I've ever seen him do that. He has the kind of laugh that makes you want to join in. It's a stupid thing to notice, but I do.

"He's gone," I blurt out.

"Who is?"

"My father. He got up and left one day just over two months ago and my mother's going to find him." Terrance stares at me. "She *is*. Jane said, plus I wished on it back at the lake." I look away, at Tiffany talking to another little girl her age. She finds friends wherever we go. "And now I'm stuck here. Okay?"

"This place isn't all that bad," he says, still smiling.

Maybe not.

Twenty-One

I T'S only the second day of Camp Jesus Saves and already Tiffany is talking about not going. She's like a marble in a tin can, bouncing off every corner of our room, running from me and the hairbrush. The only article of clothing she has agreed to put on is a pair of mismatched socks. And downstairs Great-Aunt Grace is yelling at us to come on down to breakfast before she has to come up.

"You're asking for it, Tiffany."

Footsteps on the stairs.

"See what you did."

Great-Aunt Grace stops in the doorway and seems to fill it up. It's not even nine in the morning and she's already got a cigarette and an attitude. Her big hands find her hips. "Why isn't this child dressed?"

Tiffany is over by the window, hiding behind a sheer curtain.

"She said she doesn't want to go to camp." I wave my hands in front of my face, wafting smoke.

"She ain't got a choice in the matter. Girl, come out and get your narrow behind dressed before I dress it for you."

Tiffany stamps her mismatched feet. "No," she says, but with a whole lot less sass.

"All right, then, girl, you brought me to it."

Great-Aunt Grace comes all the way into our room and goes straight for Tiffany's bed. She takes a drag on her cigarette and grabs Mr. Teddy Daniels. Tiffany bursts out from behind her curtain, arms flailing. Great-Aunt Grace holds the bear high above her head. It might as well be on top of the Empire State Building. Tiffany wilts.

"Get dressed and I'll give your raggedy bear back." Great-Aunt Grace starts for the door.

"You can't take him!" Tiffany stomps her feet again. "It's not nice!" she shouts, and it's not. Taking a kid's bear hostage is low, but when Great-Aunt Grace leaves, Mr. Teddy D. tucked firmly in the crick of her arm, Tiffany lets me get her dressed and do her hair. Then she takes off, about to go flying downstairs. I grab her by the arm.

"What's wrong with you?"

Tiffany tries to yank her arm free. I hold it tighter. "I hate it here," she says. "Do you know what happened at camp yesterday? I made two friends, Dominique and Jackie, and Jackie asked me why am I staying with Great-Aunt Grace and they both said she's crazy, and I said I know, and then they asked me where Mommy and Daddy were and I told them that Mommy went to find Daddy and they said, 'Where's he at?' and I said we don't know, and they said, 'Is he lost?' and I said I don't know, and Jackie said if he is, what if he wants to stay that way?" Tiffany takes a deep breath. "What if it's true? What if Daddy wants to stay lost?"

"He doesn't."

Tiffany rubs her eyes. I don't think either of us has had a good night's sleep since we got here. "Where do you think he went, then?"

Dad and I played a game of "What if?" a few weeks before he left. Dad started off small, like he always did: "What if you were bald-headed?"

I replied, "I'd ask Ms. Elliott in 4D if I could borrow one of her wigs."

"Okay, now, what if you could shed your life and become something new? What would you be?"

I didn't understand the question.

Dad stood up, like he was agitated or excited — I couldn't tell which. "It's like this." He slipped out of his jacket and let it fall to the floor. "Shed this life like an old coat. What if you could do that? What would you be?"

A princess, a millionaire, a lion tamer. By the time we were done, Dad had shed his life and become a pilot, just so he could get out there and see the world. Now I wonder if that's what he did this time, shed his life with us and stepped into a new one. But then I remember what he said to Mom right before he left.

"He went to find the perfect place for us," I say now.

"Okay, what's it like?"

I close my eyes and try to call up the image, the one I've had for so long. "It's a whole house to ourselves—not an apartment—and every inch of it is filled with light. It always smells good, like laundry detergent, and—"

"Do I get my own room, so I don't have to listen to you snore?"

My eye snap open. "I don't snore."

"You do," Tiffany says. "So loud."

"Whatever. You'll have your own room."

"Is it purple?"

"The purplest."

Together we build this place until it becomes so real, we could almost crawl inside it. Then we go down to the kitchen, where Great-Aunt Grace is standing at the stove, Mr. Teddy Daniels still tucked under her arm. She gives Tiffany a head-to-toe look before handing him over. Tiffany snatches him and glares. Great-Aunt Grace hands her a bowl of grits.

"You too big to be cryin' over that raggedy bear."

"He's not raggedy; he just needs his changes of clothes," Tiffany retorts, taking her seat.

"Changin' his clothes ain't gonna change the fact that you too big to be carryin' a bear around, girl," Great-Aunt Grace says.

Tiffany starts kicking her chair—*thwack, thwack, thwack*—until I place my hand on her leg. She stops. Great-Aunt Grace goes over to the window where Mr. Shuffle is perched and looks out into her backyard.

"Tiffany, come on and feed this cat."

"You know what else is great about the perfect place?" I whisper to Tiffany, as she rises slowly from her seat.

"What?"

"There's no Gag."

~~~~~~~~~

Instead of eating with Dominique and Jackie, Tiffany sits with me at lunch.

"Is it going better today?" I ask.

She nods. "We made fans in arts and crafts, but I drew a picture of the perfect place instead. Wanna see?" Tiffany reaches into her backpack and pulls out a picture of a boxy blue house with a yellow door and five windows. She's drawn the four of us on the front lawn, holding hands.

"We have a dog?" I ask, pointing at the brown, four-legged blob sprawled on the ground in front of us. Tiffany nods. "I'm allergic to dogs."

"You'll deal. Here comes your boyfriend."

"Terrance is not my boyfriend."

"Then why is he always walking us to Great-Aunt Grace's store and sitting with you at lunch? And you're always writing down words for him?"

"Both those things happened *once* and that was yesterday, and it's because we don't know the way from here. Also, for the record, I've only written down two words for him." Two on the walk home yesterday, that is, in addition to *rudimentary*. I gave Terrance two more words in Bible study yesterday, too, and one in arts and crafts today, but Tiffany doesn't need to know all that.

Terrance jogs over to us, his book bag like a boulder on his back. "Oh, hey, Tiffany."

"You got ketchup on your shirt," Tiffany tells him.

Which is truly amazing, considering Terrance hasn't even bitten into his hot dog yet. He sits down across from us and digs in. Within seconds, ketchup is everywhere. I hand him a napkin. "Thanks." He licks his fingers clean. "Did I tell you I think I've perfected the design for my time machine?"

"You're building a time machine? What for?" Tiffany asks.

"So I can go back in time and warn the black people in Africa about the ships on the horizon. It's the least I can do."

"They'd need more than a warning," I say. "They'd need weapons. What good is foresight if you don't have a gun?"

Terrance considers this as he jams the straw into his

juice box. "I'm not sure I can take all that stuff back in time with me. I may not even be able to wear clothes."

"You're going naked?" Tiffany asks. Her eyes bug out of her head. She covers her face with her drawing. "Ew! That's so gross!"

"Thanks, Tiffany," Terrance says.

"Maybe you should go back in time to whenever Jaguar started calling you Yuck Mouth," I say. "What's that about anyway?"

"Oh, this one time when I—"

But we never get to find out, because Jaguar tramples Terrance's words with her own. "Yoo-hoo, lover birds!"

She's on us in moments. Jaguar nudges Pamela with her elbow, knocking sunflower seeds from Pamela's cupped hand.

"We're not lovers," I say flatly.

"Of course you are. Why else are you together all the time?"

"All the time is a gross exaggeration," Terrance says, balling up his napkins and tossing them on his Styrofoam plate.

Tiffany squints up at Jaguar, taking her in. "You're a bad person," she says, and looks her up and down, from the top of Jaguar's ponytailed head to her neon orange toes. "The worst person in the whole wide world." I reach over and squeeze Tiffany's hand in mine. Tiffany scowls at me and tries to pull away.

Jaguar snatches Tiffany's drawing off the table and holds it up between two fingers. "What's this?"

"The perfect place for us," Tiffany says. "And *just* us."

"Who's 'us'?" Jaguar asks.

"Me, Mommy, Daddy, and Jeanie."

"And where exactly are your mommy and daddy?" Jaguar asks sweetly. "Did they die?"

Pamela sucks in her breath. I squeeze Tiffany's hand again, harder this time. She yanks it free and stands up to take Jaguar head on. She's barely up to Jaguar's waist. "They're not dead, *you bad person.* Our father went away and our mother is looking for him. When she finds him, we're gonna move into the perfect place." Tiffany snatches her picture back.

Jaguar sticks out her bottom lip in mock sympathy. "Isn't that the saddest thing you've ever heard, Pam?"

Pamela shrugs. "Whatever. Let's just go," she mutters.

Since Jaguar won't take Pamela's advice, I do. I get up and start gathering my things. Then I take Tiffany's hand and turn to take my trash to the garbage can, barely a foot away, when Jaguar says, "There's no such thing as a perfect place, and you're stupid for believing there is." The words are like a hand on my shoulder, whirling me around so I'm right back where I started, only stunned.

"Tell her she's wrong, Jeanie," Tiffany says, her voice quivering.

"Yeah, tell me I'm wrong and that you didn't make it

up." Jaguar squints at me. "Why are you breathing like that?"

My inhaler is in the small pocket of my backpack, but I won't reach for it in front of Jaguar. I want to walk—no, run, sprout wings so I can take flight, but I can't move. The whistle blows, signaling the end of lunch. Kids go careening across the lawn on their way to who knows where, and still I'm standing here even as Jaguar loses interest and starts telling Pamela how excited she is to be spending August in Florida with her aunt.

I find my voice. "If you want heat, you may as well just go to—"

"Let's go, Jeanie," Terrance cuts in. "We have Bible study."

"Wait," Jaguar growls. "Was she going to tell me to go to hell?"

"Yes," I tell her. "It would be less humid."

"It would," Terrance agrees. "Dry heat. Probably a lot like Phoenix."

"You think you're so much smarter than everyone else," Jaguar says. "But you're just a nappy-headed loser whose parents don't even want her."

My heart starts to sprint.

"Ow, Jeanie!" Tiffany yelps. I had her hand in a death grip and didn't even notice. She pulls away, I put my lunch tray down, and now I've got two free hands, both clenched into fists.

"Oh, yeah? Well, you're just a fake, phony pain in the butt who's so pathetic she has to bully her way into a candy store and make a mess." With each word, I jab the air with my index finger right in front of Jaguar's chest. She takes a step closer to me, and my finger bounces off of her flesh.

Jaguar lets loose a cry like a cat caught under a rocking chair and lunges at me. I go flying backward, right into the nearest garbage can. It goes down with me, and soon Jaguar and I are rolling around in apple cores, balled-up napkins, and half sandwiches. I grab a handful of her hair and yank it as hard as I can. She repays me with a thump to the forehead that makes little white lights dance before my eyes. She goes for my neck; I go for her face. All the while I'm vaguely aware of a chant beginning, low at first and then loud as rushing water.

"Fight! Fight! Fight!"

I freeze, aware now of a crowd gathering. Jaguar takes this opportunity to mush me in my forehead, pushing me toward the ground and smearing my hair in the trash. I pick up a handful of garbage and shove it in her face.

Suddenly everything goes quiet.

"Stop it! Stop it at once!"

Faster than Eunetta can get to us, Jaguar flings herself away from me and slumps over. She begins to whimper.

"Liar!" Tiffany cries, rushing forward. "She started it. She hit my sister first!"

There is red pulsating beneath Eunetta's ten layers of makeup. "Up. The both of you come with me. *Now!*"

Jaguar and I get to our feet and follow Eunetta. She leads us to the small, air-conditioned guidance counselor's office she's taken over for the summer. Jaguar enters first, and then me. As I walk past Eunetta, she grabs my arm and whispers so that only I can hear.

"I knew you were gonna be trouble."

Twenty-Two

W ELL, this simply will not do."

Eunetta is pacing, her hands behind her back. Her wig is more lopsided than usual and she's working overtime chewing a stick of gum.

"This is Camp Jesus Saves, for God's sake!" She stops in the middle of her office, and though she's supposed to be talking to the both of us, she's only looking at me.

"She put her hands on me first," Jaguar says, jerking her thumb at me.

"It was an accident."

"How do you hit someone by accident?" Eunetta asks. She's incredulous.

"I didn't hit her. I was going like this to make my points"—I demonstrate—"and she walked right into my finger. Then she went buckwild."

Eunetta shakes her head. "Jaguar, you should know better than to allow yourself to be provoked in this way.

You're a good Christian girl with good Christian values. Your daddy's the pastor, for God's sake."

I almost implode. "Pastor Burroughs is your father?" Jaguar and Eunetta stare at me. "I guess I'm the only one who finds the irony staggering," I say, using one of Dad's favorite expressions.

"You are," Eunetta says flatly. I wait for my speech about being better than fighting, but what I get is, "You can't help the blood you're born into."

The blood I was born into boils as whatever is in my hair starts to drip down my neck. I reach up and touch it. Ketchup. I open my mouth to tell Eunetta all about Jaguar's good Christian values, but then I close it just as quick. It's not like she'd believe me anyway. She made up her mind about me the minute she found out I was related to Great-Aunt Grace.

Great-Aunt Grace.

There's a cell phone on Eunetta's desk. I watch her for any sign that she's getting ready to use it, but she shakes her head again. She's stopped pacing, too, and she's no longer jawing her gum. Maybe, just maybe, if I keep my mouth shut, she'll calm down and let us off with a warning. And if she does, I'm planning on scooping up Tiffany, walking out the front door of Camp Jesus Saves, and never looking back.

"Of course I'll have to call both of your homes."

"What?" Jaguar blurts.

I can't even get my mouth to work. We're both sitting here covered in food. We've rolled through garbage. Isn't that punishment enough? When she dropped us off, Great-Aunt Grace told us not to act up today; she said the same thing yesterday. And now she'll be getting a phone call about me fighting. Despite the air conditioning in Eunetta's office, I'm starting to sweat. So is Jaguar. She fans herself.

Eunetta says she will make those calls while we're here in her office. "Who's first for the firing squad?"

Neither Jaguar nor I answer.

"Jeanie, how about you?"

My mouth's still not working. I let out a sound that's half squeak, half grunt. Even though Jaguar is about to get a phone call home too, a smirk is playing on her lips as Eunetta picks up her cell, ready to dial.

"Grace is at that store of hers right now, isn't she?"

I stay silent. No way I'm offering up any information right about now. Eunetta doesn't need me to. She takes a telephone book down from a shelf behind her desk and flips to the G's. She's got the number for Grace's Goodies in no time, and makes sure to put the call on speaker.

"Yes?"

Great-Aunt Grace sounds like she's not happy about being interrupted.

"Hello, Grace. It's Eunetta. Fancy that we're chatting so soon." Eunetta's voice is like melted butter. I could gladly kick her in both shins. She laughs a stupid little laugh and pauses for dramatic effect.

Great-Aunt Grace doesn't disappoint. "Just tell me what those kids did and don't leave nothing out!"

"Not kids. Jeanie," Eunetta replies, and she does not disappoint, either. By the time she's finished telling on me, Great-Aunt Grace is breathing like she ran up ten flights of stairs two steps at a time.

"Is she there? Can she hear me?"

"She's here."

"You listen to me, girl, and you listen good. I'm on my way and you best believe I got something in store for you!"

Before Eunetta can say anything else, Great-Aunt Grace hangs up, the sound of the dial tone lingering in the air, low and ominous, like a threat.

~~~~~~~

Great-Aunt Grace does not come quietly. During Jaguar's phone call home, I'm parked in a chair outside of Eunetta's office, and I hear my great-aunt well before I see her. She turns the corner and barrels down the hallway like a tank into battle, kids running to get out of her way. Moon is behind her, struggling to keep up.

"Girl, you done it now!" Great-Aunt Grace roars. She's moving at the speed of light.

In my mind a voice says, *Run!* But it's too late. Great-Aunt Grace is in my face now, her index finger pointing right at my nose. Some kids nearby have begun to stare.

"I had to close up shop to come down here and get you, girl. You costin' me money! But you ain't gonna cost me a bit more of my time." Her eyes alight on one of the boys in the audience. "Find me Tiffany Daniels, and don't you dare drag your feet."

It's likely the kid has no idea who Tiffany is, but when Great-Aunt Grace talks, folks listen. He takes off. Moments later he returns with Tiffany, who's struggling to carry my backpack and hers. She looks up at me, her eyes asking a million questions. I just shake my head and hold my hand out for my bag.

"Let's go," Great-Aunt Grace barks. Then she turns on Moon and says, "*This* is why I didn't want kids."

I keep my eyes on the ground as I follow Great-Aunt Grace and Moon to his car. This is one fight I don't have a chance of winning. I slide into the back seat. Great-Aunt Grace slams her door so hard, Moon mutters, "Baby, take it easy on Betty. She ain't much longer for this world."

"Shut up, Moon," Great-Aunt Grace snaps.

"Will do."

The ride home feels longer than the one from Jersey to Black Lake. Moon turns on the radio, tries to encourage a sing-along—to break up some of the tension in the car, I guess. Great-Aunt Grace turns the radio off. We drive the rest of the way in silence.

When we pull up to Great-Aunt Grace's house, I take my time getting out of the car. My mind is racing faster than my heart. What has Great-Aunt Grace planned? Maybe she's going to go to the back to get a switch. I heard that's how they do things in the South. No. She goes up the steps and through the front door.

"Good luck, girl," Moon says to me as he gets out of the car. "She really ain't one to mess with." He starts up the road on foot.

"Thanks for the warning," I call after him, sarcastic as you please.

I trudge to the front steps and into the house. Great-Aunt Grace is already in the kitchen, taking out some of her anger on the pots and pans.

"Treasure, get in here," she says.

I drop my backpack on the living room floor and go into the kitchen. Three of the four burners on the stove are lit. Great-Aunt Grace is opening a bottle of vegetable oil. When she sees me, she nods at the corner near the back door.

"Go stand over there."

"I need to take a shower. There's ketchup in my hair."

"Go stand over there."

"But—"

Great-Aunt Grace gives me the full heat of her glare. I go stand in the corner.

"Now get on your knees."

"What?"

"And stay there."

"For how long?"

"Until you get it through your hard head that you best keep your hands to yourself and do what I say. I reckon your knees will be pretty sore by the time that happens."

"She hit me first, and she wrecked your store!" I add that last part hoping Great-Aunt Grace will ease up, thinking I fought this battle for her.

"If you think I need you to take up my cause, girl, you are truly as simple as you look."

"This is child abuse!"

"On your knees!"

I do as I'm told.

"I'm telling my mother."

"Go ahead," says Great-Aunt Grace. "Make sure you tell her about the fight. Oh, and don't forget to mention all the talkin' back you do. If you gonna do some tellin', may as well tell the truth."

My knees are already starting to hurt. I grit my teeth. I won't beg to get up and give Great-Aunt Grace the satisfaction. I listen as she plops saucepans down on the stove. I've heard the sounds of her cooking enough to know that when she grunts a bit it's because she's getting the big cast-iron skillet from the bottom cabinet.

"Tiffany!" she calls.

Tiffany doesn't respond.

"Tiffany!" Great-Aunt Grace bellows like a walrus this time.

Tiffany scrambles down the stairs and into the kitchen, looking more scared than that time she snuck and watched that movie about the killer dolls on cable.

"Treasure, get your eyes on that wall!"

"I was good at camp today," Tiffany says. "You can call Eunetta and ask."

"Ain't nobody lookin' to punish you, girl. Just set the table."

Tiffany breathes a sigh of relief. "Should I set a place for Moon? He left, but his car's still here."

"Yeah, he'll be back. Walked on over to the convenience store for some smokes. Didn't want to waste his gas."

Great-Aunt Grace starts for the living room, muttering something about Moon being cheap enough to bargain shop in a dollar store.

My knees are on fire. Mom and Dad used to say we shouldn't hate. I don't care what they say. I hate Great-Aunt Grace. I hate her, I hate her, I hate her. I hate her house, too, especially her hard kitchen floor that's covered with grit. It's a good thing Great-Aunt Grace didn't have any kids of her own, because they'd probably hate her too.

I grit my teeth against the pain. But the ache in my knees is not going anywhere. I take a deep breath in through my nose and blow it out through my mouth, but the tight feeling in my chest isn't going away either. I close my eyes and concentrate on breathing, in and out, in and out.

I want to go home.

Where's home?

In and out, in and out.

It's not fair. A girl as rotten as Jaguar gets to have a home. A good home too, I bet, with two parents who both stay put.

In and out, in and out.

And I'm stuck here with Great-Aunt Grace.

"I can't breathe."

Tiffany runs over to me, just as Great-Aunt Grace comes back from the living room.

I press my forehead against the cool surface of the tiled kitchen wall. "I can't breathe," I say again, loud enough for Great-Aunt Grace to hear.

"What are you talking about, can't breathe?" she says. "Let me find out I got an actress on my hands."

I'm wheezing now.

"She's not acting," Tiffany says. "She's having an asthma attack. She needs her inhaler!"

Tiffany runs into the living room, where I dropped my backpack, and returns with my inhaler. She hands it to me. I take one puff, two, and close my eyes while I wait for the medicine to take effect.

I don't have to open my eyes to know that Great-Aunt Grace has leaned down and is now peering closely at me. Her breath is warm on the side of my face.

"Maybe you weren't actin' this time," she says gruffly. "I don't know much about this asthma. How did she get it?"

"She was born with it," Tiffany says.

"And what makes it act up like this?"

"She was mad. When she gets mad, she gets sick."

"And," I put in loudly, now that I can speak, "it's aggravated by pet dander, dust, *and* cigarette smoke. You've pretty much got all three covered in this house." I turn around to face Great-Aunt Grace. She glares at me. "Mom was supposed to talk to you about it. Did she?"

"She may have mentioned it, but I can't go rearrangin' my life at a drop of a hat, girl."

"Can I get up now?"

"Suppose so, but you gotta go upstairs to your room and do some further thinkin' about what you done."

I go upstairs, take a shower, then go to my room but I don't do any thinking. I fall asleep.

Hours later I roll over in my bed and stare up at the ceiling. It's late. I slept right through dinner, which is fine by me because whatever it was, I'm sure Great-Aunt Grace burnt it to a crisp.

The door opens. Great-Aunt Grace comes in and turns on the light. Tiffany squirms in her sleep but doesn't wake up. Great-Aunt Grace has a plate in one hand and a glass of water in the other. She comes over to my bed and puts the plate on the nightstand next to me. It's piled high with two pork chops smothered in gravy, white rice, and corn. It smells okay, and it doesn't look burnt. . . . My stomach rumbles. I won't eat it in front of her.

She holds out the glass of water to me.

"I'm not going back to that camp," I tell her.

Great-Aunt Grace's sneakers squeak a little as she shifts from one foot back to the other. "Okay. You all right, girl?"

Of course I'm not all right. And it's all Great-Aunt Grace's fault. I shake my head, grab the water, and gulp it down. Great-Aunt Grace takes the empty glass from my outstretched hand and turns to go.

"Well, you did it to yourself, you know," she says.

"You helped."

Great-Aunt Grace doesn't turn around.

I make sure she's good and gone before I inhale my dinner, every last bite of it. And it's good, too. Looks like one of my wishes yesterday at the lake came true.

I lie down again and my eyes close immediately. Sometime in the night, I hear footsteps and feel the bed sink as someone sits down next to me. A rough hand on my fore-head, and then the weight of someone's head on my chest as they listen to me breathe. It is not until the footsteps are near the door that I force my eyes open, just in time to see Great-Aunt Grace slip out of our room and into the hallway.

Twenty-Three

THE next morning, I open my eyes to see Great-Aunt Grace standing over me, this time holding her ancient cordless phone.

"It's your mama," she says, thrusts the phone at me, and leaves.

Mom doesn't even let me say hello before she shrieks, "You got into a fight?"

I glance at the clock. It's barely nine in the morning and Great-Aunt Grace has already snitched. "Gag made me have an asthma attack."

"She didn't. You got yourself worked up, as usual. Now, why were you fighting?"

"Because this girl, Jaguar, said something mean to Tiffany."

At the sound of her name, Tiffany stirs and wakes all the way up, blinking hard. "Who're you talking to?"

"Mom."

Tiffany flies across the room and snatches the phone. I

don't put up a fight. "Hi, Mommy! Did you find Daddy yet?" Tiffany frowns. "I don't know how to put it on speaker."

She hands me the phone. I don't want to press the speaker button, but I do. Mom picks up right where she left off.

"What did the girl say?"

"What girl?" asks Tiffany.

"The girl your sister fought."

"Oh, her," Tiffany says, and then the dramatics start. She recounts the fight, word for word, hit for hit. By the time Tiffany's done, Jaguar is the most deficient human being on the planet and I am the hero to trump all heroes.

"There *is* such a thing as the perfect place for us and Daddy is looking for it. That's why he left," Tiffany says.

"Is that right?" Mom says. She sounds far away. I hear a horn honk in the background.

"It is. Jeanie even talked to a sidekick and the sidekick said that Daddy is in our future as long as we don't stop believing that we'll find him."

"A 'sidekick'?" Mom sounds bewildered.

"A psychic, not a sidekick," I put in. Then I tell Mom what Jane told me. "She said happiness is in our future, and we can't have that without Dad, right?"

Mom is quiet for a good long while. She's been gone for days now. We've been talking for ten minutes, and she still hasn't mentioned anything about finding Dad.

"You can't give up hope," I tell her.

"I'm doubling back to Boydon, North Carolina, because he hasn't used the card since, but—"

My eyes meet Tiffany's. If Mom gives up hope, so will she. "Mom, don't give up hope," I say again, more firmly this time.

Mom sighs. "Okay." She pauses, but when she speaks again, her voice is just as sad and flat as before. I remember Jane's words: Happiness doesn't come easy; you have to be willing to fight for it. Suddenly, I know what I have to do.

"Let's get off this phone before Grace starts talking about you running up her bill," Mom says. Then she says a bunch of stuff about us behaving ourselves and ends with, "You two got that?"

Tiffany says, "Yes."

"I got it," I say, even though I didn't. What I do have is a plan.

~~~~~~

Since I refuse to return to Camp Jesus Saves and Tiffany won't go back without me, it'll be business as usual: breakfast and then a full day of work at Grace's Goodies. We find Great-Aunt Grace and Moon in the kitchen. He's sitting at the table, sipping from a can of soda, as Great-Aunt Grace wipes down the kitchen counter with broad, quick strokes.

Something is missing. I look around. There's Mr. Shuffle, perched on the windowsill, looking like an overstuffed black trash bag. There's the newspaper on the kitchen table, open to the word find, and Great-Aunt Grace, leaning against the counter and chomping on something—hard.

What's missing is smoke. Not a tendril of it hovers in the air.

"Well, don't just stand there gapin'," Great-Aunt Grace says to us. "Tiffany, feed Mr. Shuffle. Treasure, set the table."

When she speaks, I see a big wad of chewing gum rolling around in her mouth like a lone T-shirt tumbling in the dryer. There's no smoke because she's not smoking.

"What's with the gum?" I ask, even though I know.

"Nothin'. Just ran out of smokes."

I hide my smile as Great-Aunt Grace reaches into the silverware drawer and hands me forks, knives, and spoons. Tiffany opens up a can of wet food for Mr. Shuffle. Moon grunts a "Good morning" at us.

"My leg is actin' up again, Gracie," he says.

Great-Aunt Grace stirs the grits and says, "Been to the doctor?"

"Not since that first time. Nothin' he can do about it really, but put me back on those pills. Damn things made me sick as a dog."

Tiffany and I take our seats at the table. She quietly points out the word *faith* nestled in the letters of Great-Aunt Grace's word find. I find *tiger* and *comeuppance*. We do this silently until Great-Aunt Grace comes over and spoons steaming grits into both our bowls. Then she spits her gum into the trash and eats her grits standing up. Moon either isn't hungry or isn't ready to stop talking about his leg. He doesn't eat anything. He goes from his leg to his heart trouble and high blood pressure to the headaches he gets only in the fall. And all the while he's talking, his hand is reaching into his pocket, feeling around for something. He finally pulls out a pack of cigarettes and an orange lighter. Great-Aunt Grace is focused on her grits, but when she hears that lighter flick, her head snaps up. Moon looks at her and shrugs.

"Stress," he says.

"What did I tell you?"

"I said I got stress, woman!"

"And then what? You gonna have another?"

"Don't see why not. Some of us is temporary, while others is permanent."

Great-Aunt Grace stares at Moon long and hard. Something's going on here, but I can't tell what. This is the first time I've ever seen Moon stand up to Great-Aunt Grace. She responds by taking an ashtray from the top of the refrigerator and slamming it down on the table in front of him. Then she turns to Tiffany and me.

"Let's go. We got thangs to do."

"What about the dishes?" I ask.

Great-Aunt Grace tells me they can wait. "Get dressed

and get back down here in five minutes—or else I'm comin' up."

We meet Great-Aunt Grace at the front door in five minutes flat, sweaty and winded. She has an empty fold-up shopping cart with her. We leave Moon sitting in the kitchen, working on cigarette number two. Or three.

Great-Aunt Grace's expression is grim as we walk. Dot is outside sweeping her walkway. When she sees the three of us passing by, she shakes her head and scowls.

"Dot's still suspicious of you," I say.

Great-Aunt Grace looks back over her shoulder at Dot and then quickly away. "I ain't got time to be worried about that fool. I got thangs to do."

Tiffany and I have to just about jog to keep up with Great-Aunt Grace. By the time we make it to downtown Black Lake, sweat is pouring down my face and into my eyes.

"You're walking too fast," Tiffany complains.

Either Great-Aunt Grace didn't hear her or she doesn't care. She keeps up the same rapid clip as we cross at the intersection of Main and Ridge. Byron comes walking toward us with the girl from church. He calls out, "Morning, Ms. Washington," and waits for the three of us to approach him. But Great-Aunt Grace just passes right on by, grunting something that sounds like hello. Tiffany and I stop, trying to make up for Great-Aunt Grace's rudeness.

"What's with her today?" Byron asks.

"She's on a mission," I reply, and he laughs.

"I heard she got into it with the sheriff." He shakes his head. "Ms. Washington is all types of crazy."

The girl is hanging all over Byron just like Sasha was, only this girl is taller, more legs than torso, showing more skin than clothes. She's wearing short white shorts and a red T-shirt with an elephant walking through a triangle on the front of it. Tiffany sizes her up.

"You look different," Tiffany says.

"Different from what?" the girl asks.

"Different from Sunday, I guess. We saw you at church," I say quickly. "I'm Jeanie and this is my sister Tiffany."

"I'm Keyana, Byron's girl," she says, as if that's part of her name.

Tiffany is still staring up at Keyana, this time at the design on her shirt.

"I'm a Delta," Keyana says, pointing at the elephant. Tiffany gazes at her blankly. "It's a sorority at Howard. We collect elephants for good luck."

"Oh," Tiffany says. "Sasha collects jewelry."

"Who's—"

Byron breaks out into a fit of coughing. I grab Tiffany by the collar of her shirt and pull her away. "See you around!" I call out over my shoulder.

"Get off me!" Tiffany rages.

I don't let her go until we're inside Grace's Goodies. Tiffany rubs her neck.

"Sorry," I say, but Tiffany won't settle for anything less than a hit.

"On the leg or the arm, not the face," I warn her.

She's cocking her arm back to pop me good when Great-Aunt Grace emerges from the stockroom. "What are you two fools doin'?"

"Jeanie dragged me here by my shirt and almost choked me to death."

"She was getting ready to tell Keyana about Sasha."

"Oh, that *was* Keyana Douglas," Great-Aunt Grace says. "Thought I recognized her. She's as big a fool as the rest of them." Great-Aunt Grace pats her pants pockets, checking for her keys. "All right, now, listen to me and listen good: I got a calling that I just can't ignore. So while I'm out, I'm trustin' the two of you to keep my door locked this time." She points at me. "You keep workin' on them shelves. I'm gonna fetch you a face mask so you can't use dust as an excuse."

Great-Aunt Grace bends to look beneath the counter for the face mask. Tiffany reaches over and pops me on the leg.

"Ow! You happy now?" I ask, rubbing my stinging thigh.

Great-Aunt Grace finds the mask and tosses it on the counter. "Well, come on and get to it, girl."

I trudge around the counter, snatch up the mask, and stop just inside the doorway to the stockroom, taking my sweet time putting the mask on.

"Now, Tiffany, I got a job for you. First I want you to label something for me. Then I want you to straighten the racks."

Great-Aunt Grace comes toward me, stopping short of the entrance to the stockroom. She bends down over the box containing her security system and opens it. Everything inside the box is wrapped up in plastic.

"Take this," she says, shoving a tape at Tiffany along with a package of labels. "Put this past Sunday's date on that. Write neat as you can."

Who in the world labels a blank tape?

Great-Aunt Grace heads to the door. She stops just in front of it and stares out into the street. "Gonna be a storm," she says, and over her shoulder to me, "Treasure, you got a job to do, so stop peekin' around that corner and get to it." She leaves, locking the door behind her.

I stomp toward the shelves, but I've got no intention of cleaning a single one of them. I wait until Tiffany is busy with that label. Then I walk right over to the phone on the wall in the corner and rip the mask off my face.

In all the time I've spent in this stockroom, the phone has never rung. Does it even work? It has to.

I pick it up and hold it to my ear.

It works.

I picture the sign again. APARTMENT'S FOR RENT. FOR MORE INFORMATION CALL BROWN & ASSOCIATES AT 973-627-3746.

I punch in the number to Mr. Brown's office. A woman answers on the second ring. "Brown and Associates, how may I help you?"

"I'd like to speak to Mr. Brown, please."

"Is this his grandbaby?"

"No. It's Jeanie Daniels. He might know me as Treasure. My family and I used to live in Apartment 2F. Is he there?"

"He is, but he doesn't have time to be talking to kids."

I can't give up now. "Please. Just ask him."

"Hang on."

The woman places me on hold, leaving me alone with a recorded voice telling me that Brown & Associates is a family-run business that's been around since 1987.

"Hello?"

"Mr. Brown?"

"Yeah. Who is this and what do you want?"

"It's Jeanie Daniels. I used to live in Apartment 2F. Remember?"

"Yeah. Your mama skipped out on three months' worth of rent, and sent me half of it about a week ago." He pauses. "What are you, kid, like, ten? What're you calling me about this for?"

"I'm twelve, actually, and I'm calling because my father left us a few months before we snuck out—that's why we didn't have the rent money—and now my mother is trying to find him, but we've got nothing to go on and I was wondering—well, I was wondering if he'd called looking for us and maybe when he couldn't get in touch with us at the old apartment, he called you and mentioned where he was and—"

"He didn't."

"Oh."

"Listen, kid, I got work to do. When you talk to your mama, tell her—"

"What about the mail?"

"Huh?"

"Maybe he wrote us. Where's our mail from the past week?"

"Still piled up in your box. I haven't found another tenant yet."

I take a deep breath. "Do you think you could . . . check the mail for me and see if he wrote to us?"

"Who do you think I am, kid? Some errand boy?"

"Please. I'm begging you."

There's silence on the other end.

"Please," I say again. "And if my dad did write to us, will you hold on to the letter for me? I'll call back tomorrow."

"Tomorrow? Do you know how busy I am? I'll get to that mailbox when I'm free, and I'll call you when I feel like it."

"But the mailbox is right in the building where you

live. You just—please. If we don't find him, we'll be home-less."

Mr. Brown sighs. "All right, kid. I'll check your mail-box today or tomorrow. Day after that at the latest. In the meantime, don't be blowing up my phone, calling every hour on the hour. When I get your mail, I'll call you. I have your number right here on my caller ID. Got it, kid?"

"Yeah. I got it."

Mr. Brown hangs up before I can say thank you or goodbye. I don't care. He said he could get to our mailbox in a day; two, tops. I sit down on the cold stockroom floor, hope pumping like blood in my veins.

Twenty-Four

GREAT-AUNT Grace returns an hour later with her shopping cart full of plastic bags, all knotted at the top so their contents won't spill out. What the heck is Great-Aunt Grace hiding? I stare at the bags, thinking I should have wished for x-ray vision when I was skipping stones at the lake.

"What's in them?" Tiffany asks.

"Mind your business," Great-Aunt Grace replies. For the remainder of the day she guards that shopping cart like it's got bags of gold in it. When we get back to her house, she puts the bags in the hall closet.

"No snooping," she says, and starts fixing dinner.

We don't snoop, but we sure enough do guess.

"Are there presents for us in the bags?" Tiffany asks.

Great-Aunt Grace humphs. "Yeah, sure. And Mr. Shuffle will be makin' breakfast in the mornin'."

That might be an improvement.

"Is it stuff for cleaning?" I ask. "This place could use a good scrub-down."

Great-Aunt Grace shakes her head. "Y'all just best forget about what's in them bags if you know what's good for you."

By the time we're done eating and I finish the dishes, the storm Great-Aunt Grace predicted is brewing outside. I run upstairs to our room, put on my pajamas, and jump into bed. Tiffany's right behind me. I'm hoping to be cutting z's long before the thunder starts. I'm just closing my eyes, ready for a good, long sleep when—*BAM!*

That's not thunder. It's the front door slamming, followed by a loud voice. Moon.

He's complaining, as usual, only this time at the top of his lungs. About cigarettes.

I put my finger to my lips.

"I'm on a spy mission. Solo," I tell Tiffany. She pouts, but she stays where she is. I creep down the stairs, quiet as a mouse wearing socks. If I stand in the downstairs bathroom, I can peek out the door and see and hear everything going on in the kitchen, where Moon and Great-Aunt Grace are arguing.

"How in the sweet name of Jesus can every single store sell out of the same cigarette at the same time? Good Lord, I need a smoke."

Great-Aunt Grace's voice is calm. "Jesus and his daddy

ain't got a thing to do with cigarettes." She's doing something with sea-green yarn, crocheting what looks like clothes for a baby. She doesn't look up from her work as she gums her gum.

It's after ten o'clock now, and I'm assuming all the stores are closed. Moon paces the floor like a caged animal. Something brushes against my heel. I almost yelp, then catch myself and cover my mouth.

"What are you doing down here?"

Tiffany says, "I'm on a solo spy mission too."

"Solo means *alone.*"

Tiffany shrugs and then says, in a voice louder than a whisper, "What'd I miss?"

My little sister is the Worst. Spy. Ever. "Keep quiet. And listen."

Tiffany scowls, but she does just that.

Great-Aunt Grace is talking now. "Guess you'll have to drive over to Moonachie tomorrow, or wait until they restock over here," she says. "Lord knows when that will be. Maybe Monday?"

"Monday is days away! Smokin' is not a hobby for me, Gracie! It ain't for you, either. Suppose I drive to Moonachie tomorrow, but what about tonight? I can feel the want down to my bones."

"Mmmm, is that right?" Great-Aunt Grace says. She still hasn't looked up, but when she does, she says, "What brand is it you smoke again?" She puts her crochet down.

"Biltons, woman, you know that. I tried some Marl-boros today and they tasted like pencil shavings!" Moon makes a spitting sound, like he's still trying to get that taste out of his mouth.

"Pencil shavings, huh?" Great-Aunt Grace says.

She puts down her crochet and, like a magician, pulls a pack of cigarettes from somewhere. Her bra? If so, I don't want to know about it. But Moon wouldn't care if she'd pulled that pack of Biltons from where the sun don't shine. He holds out his hand for them.

"What do we have here?" Great-Aunt Grace says, star-ing at the cigarettes as if they materialized from thin air.

"Let me have 'em, Grace," Moon says. He starts toward her.

"Not until we work out a deal."

Moon stops midstep and stares at her. He holds up his empty hands as if to say, "I got nothing."

Great-Aunt Grace seems to read his mind. "I don't want nothin' material. Now, if you'll recall a conversation we had this mornin', before the girls got up, I told you in plain English not to smoke around my grandniece. I told you about her sickness. And what do you do while she's sit-tin' right at the table next to you? Light one up. You ask me what I want from you, and I want this: Never smoke around Treasure again."

"Grace, this is practically my house too—"

"Never said it wasn't. But that girl is my family and you

best do right by her." Pause. "There's more where these came from, you know."

Great-Aunt Grace gets up and starts in my direction. I pull Tiffany into the darkened bathroom, but Great-Aunt Grace stops at the hall closet a few feet away. Then she heads back to the kitchen and sits down at the table again, at least half a dozen plastic bags at her feet. She reaches into one, pulls out a box, and waves it in the air. A carton of cigarettes. She rips open the box and pulls out a pack.

"I've got more in that closet, just couldn't carry 'em all out here to you."

Moon's mouth falls open. "Gracie, why you got all them Biltons?"

"Yeah, why does she?" Tiffany asks.

"Shush!"

"Wait a dang minute," Moon says slowly. "You ain't buy out all the cigarettes from all those stores, did you?"

Silence from Great-Aunt Grace, and then an explosion from Moon.

"Woman, you're off your rocker, you know that?" He keeps wiping his brow until it looks like he's going to wipe the brown clean off.

"Yes, sir," she says. "So if you want yourself a smoke tonight, you gonna have to get it from me. But I'm tellin' you, you best take it outside, down the block, away from this house while Treasure's stayin' here."

Moon doesn't say a word. He's lost the battle; that's

plain to see. But the way he keeps opening and closing his mouth tells me he's still trying to figure out a way to win. There's no such thing as winning with Great-Aunt Grace, though, and he should know this better than anyone else.

Moon holds out one hand to her for the cigarettes. Great-Aunt Grace pulls back.

"Your word."

Moons sucks his breath in through his nose and blows it out of his mouth. "You have my word."

"Good. That'll be eight-fifty."

Twenty-Five

I still can't believe Great-Aunt Grace stood up to Moon for me. No matter how many times I try to wrap my mind around it, I can't.

"Can you believe she did that?" I ask Tiffany, as we're brushing our teeth the next morning.

Tiffany rinses her mouth. Then she examines herself in the mirror. "When I grow up I'm gonna be pretty like Sasha."

"Yeah, okay. Can you believe Great-Aunt Grace did all that with Moon and the cigarettes for me? Tiffany, I'm talking to you."

Tiffany tears her eyes away from her reflection and looks up at me. "You'll be smart like Keyana."

I screw the cap back on the toothpaste and wipe my mouth on the neck of my nightshirt. "I can't be pretty too?"

"No."

"Why?"

"Because your hair is cuh-razy." Tiffany darts out of the bathroom and into the hallway before I can pop her.

She's right, though: my hair is crazy. Dad used to say it's because our hair, his and mine, is impervious to "doing"—unaffected by combs, brushes, blow dryers, and gel. No matter what you try, our hair will curl up and puff right back out. My throat tightens. It's been only a day since I called Mr. Brown and asked him to check the mail. By tomorrow, he's supposed to call me.

What if Mr. Brown doesn't find anything in the mail from Dad? What if Mom can't find him at all? We won't have anywhere to go and we'll never be an aggregate again.

I look at my reflection in the mirror, hair all over my head and eyes blinking back tears.

Don't give up hope.

I reach into the cabinet above Great-Aunt Grace's sink and find a hard bristle brush and a jar of Blue Magic hair grease. Then I get to work, slicking and brushing until I've managed to pull my hair into a ponytail. The front is laid down, but the back is still an explosion of unruly curls. I wipe my face on my nightshirt. My hair is impervious to doing, and from here on out, I'm going to be impervious to hopelessness.

~~~~~~~

I wonder if I should thank Great-Aunt Grace. She's sitting across the table from me, concentrating on her word find and chewing a wad of mint-flavored gum. If I thank her, though, she'll know I was spying, so I keep my mouth 100 percent shut. I don't complain about the dry scrambled eggs or crispy-black bacon, and when Tiffany and I are done eating, I start the dishes without being told to.

I'm scrubbing bacon grease off of Great-Aunt Grace's cast-iron skillet when the doorbell rings. Great-Aunt Grace goes to answer it. Tiffany slides into her empty seat and takes over the word find. When Great-Aunt Grace returns looking grimmer than ever, Tiffany says proudly, "I found three words."

Great-Aunt Grace ignores her and goes over to the refrigerator. She reaches up and takes down a small stack of rumpled papers. I recognize the one on top immediately: Eunetta's reward poster for her missing pearls. Great-Aunt Grace takes out the most wrinkled one of all—Dot's poster about her missing statue—and studies it.

"What's going on?" I ask, as I set the skillet in the drain board.

"Dot came over, talkin' about how Mr. and Mrs. Russell came back from Virginia Beach yesterday and found out someone broke in and stole some of Juanita's jewelry. Askin' me if I know anything about it. I swear that woman is as simple as they come. What am I gonna do with this junk?" Great-Aunt Grace jabs her index finger at the picture of Dot's elephant statue.

"Found another word!" Tiffany declares. She pumps

her fist in the air. "Earth to Great-Aunt Grace, I found another word."

When Great-Aunt Grace's gaze doesn't shift from the flier, Tiffany gets up from the table and stalks over to her. "What's that?" she demands to know, practically climbing up Great-Aunt Grace's side to get a look. "Oh," she says, losing interest almost immediately. She hops back to the table in full bunny mode. "Keyana likes elephants."

"What's that, girl?" Great-Aunt Grace says.

"Keyana likes elephants. She was wearing a shirt with an elephant on it when we met her. She said she thinks they're good luck."

"Wait," I say to Great-Aunt Grace. "You don't think Keyana—"

Great-Aunt Grace is already striding into the living room, Tiffany and me right behind her. She picks up her ancient cordless phone and dials a number.

"Sheriff Baxter?" she barks. "It's Grace Washington. I reckon I'm ready for you to search my house."

~~~~~~

Great-Aunt Grace gave Sheriff Baxter strict instructions. He is to come within the hour and by himself. He follows these orders to a T, making it to Great-Aunt Grace's house a half hour after she hung up the phone. Great-Aunt Grace is on the porch waiting for him. She makes Tiffany and me stay in the living room.

Sheriff Baxter's footsteps are heavy on the porch stairs. "So happy you saw your way to letting me in," he says as he walks through the front door and into the living room. "My Eunetta—well, you know, she doesn't give up easy. Neither does Dot—she's called me every day since we came round here the other day. I'll just take a look around."

The sheriff is big any way you look at him. He's tall and wide with broad shoulders and a big stomach hanging over his belt buckle like a terrace. His gun is holstered on his hip. He lumbers around Great-Aunt Grace's living room, dwarfing everything with his size. Great-Aunt Grace watches him in silence, her arms crossed over her chest. When he's done "searching" the living room, he and Great-Aunt Grace move on to the kitchen. Tiffany and I get up. Great-Aunt Grace tells us to stay right where we are, so we sit back down and listen to muffled voices and creaking floors until Great-Aunt Grace and Sheriff Baxter return to the living room.

"My deputy and I did check other houses, you know," Sheriff Baxter is saying. "But folks were a bit more concerned about yours, what with your record and all. I'm sure you understand."

"Yeah, I understand," Great-Aunt Grace replies flatly.

Sheriff Baxter nods to her and to us, ready to hit the road.

"Oh, and one more thing, Sheriff," Great-Aunt Grace calls.

He stops and turns to her.

"Would you mind givin' me and my grandnieces a ride over to H&H Auto Service?"

Sheriff Baxter's eyebrows furrow. "What you going there for? You don't even have a car."

"I ain't goin' about a car. I'm goin' to visit a friend. Besides, it's the least you could do, since I been so . . . cooperative."

"Well, I guess I can take you," Sheriff Baxter grumbles.

Great-Aunt Grace disappears into the kitchen and returns with her keys and a handful of papers. The fliers? We pile into Sheriff Baxter's car, Great-Aunt Grace riding shotgun and Tiffany and me in the back behind a thick pane of bulletproof glass. We look like a pair of criminals. I slide all the way down in my seat and wonder what's going on.

We pull up to H&H Auto Service a few minutes later. It's not much more than a patch of cement dotted with banged-up cars. There are a few gas pumps and a squat building with three chairs lined up out front. Sasha is sitting in one of those chairs, legs crossed, flipping through a magazine and swinging her foot.

We climb out of Sheriff Baxter's car. He guns the engine, ready to pull off.

"Hang on, Sheriff. There's someone I want you to meet."

"What are you doing? It's Keyana who likes elephants," I hiss.

Great-Aunt Grace ignores me and calls to Sasha. She looks up, shielding her eyes from the sun, squinting at Great-Aunt Grace.

"Oh!" Sasha says at last, hopping up. She bounds over in a skin-tight tank dress, bracelets jingling and everything bouncing. Sheriff Baxter's eyebrows almost shoot off his face.

"Sheriff, this is Sasha, Byron Lockett's girl. Where's he at, anyway?" Great-Aunt Grace asks, looking around.

"He's in the back, working on his motorcycle. The boss isn't here. Why? Something wrong with your car?" Sasha asks the sheriff.

"No, we here to pick up mine," Great-Aunt Grace says, pointing in the general direction of a blue car wrecked beyond repair.

Sasha frowns. "I don't think it's ready yet."

"I can see that. I'll talk to Byron about it," Great-Aunt Grace replies. "I see you got yourself a whole jewelry store there, girl."

"Oh!" Sasha's eyes light up as she jangles her armful of bracelets. "Glad you like them! I just purely love them!" She leans into us conspiratorially. "I'm not wearing the prettiest one. It's gold and about this thick." She holds her index finger and thumb an inch apart. "And it has all these different color stones in it, you know? Byron gave it to me. He doesn't like me to wear it too much, but you can't really see it unless you *see* it, you know?"

"Nah, girl, you doin' just fine describin' it," Great-Aunt Grace says, unfolding her stack of papers. She shuffles through them and holds up the reward flier with a picture of Lucinda's stolen bracelet. "Does it look like this?"

"Yes! Just like that." Sasha beams. But as she reads over the flier, her lips moving, her smile fades. "Wait. What's going on?"

"Lord only knows. Sheriff, what's goin' on?" Great-Aunt Grace says.

Sheriff Baxter climbs slowly from his cruiser. He points at the flier Great-Aunt Grace is holding up. "You're saying Byron gave you a bracelet that looks just like that?"

Sasha nods. She looks frightened.

"Do you have it right now?"

"It's at home."

"What's at home?"

We all turn at the sound of Byron's voice as he strolls over to us, his movie-star smile already in place.

"My bracelet is at home, the one you gave me. They're saying you stole it."

Byron's smile falters, but only for a moment. "Come on, Sheriff, Ms. Washington. You know me. I didn't steal anything," he says smoothly.

"Did he give you pearls, too, or an elephant statue?" Sheriff Baxter asks Sasha.

"No, I reckon he gave that statue to Keyana," Great-Aunt Grace says.

"No, I didn't," Byron says quickly, his eyes darting to Sasha.

"And who is Keyana?" Sasha demands to know.

"Girl who lives over in Thatcher," Great-Aunt Grace puts in. "Family used to own a little spot here in Black Lake called Olive's. Cobbler wasn't much to speak of, but the corn' beef was all right."

"Keyana goes to Howard," I add.

"And she loves elephants," Tiffany chimes in.

"You told me you don't have no other girls!" Sasha lunges at Byron.

"Sasha, be easy!" Byron shouts, trying to duck her blows. "Keyana doesn't mean anything to me."

"But you gave her that statue, right?" Sasha says, landing a blow on Byron's shoulder.

"Yeah, but it didn't mean anything, baby. It's you I love!"

"You lowdown, dirty thief!" Sheriff Baxter shouts. "What did you do with my wife's pearls?"

Sasha stops hitting Byron and waits for his answer. He has run out of steam. "I gave 'em to a girl over in Chesterfield," he mutters.

"And Mrs. Russell's gold necklace and ring?"

"That was gonna be for you, Sasha, baby," Byron says.

Sasha isn't having it. She lets loose with every swear

word in the world and some that haven't even been invented yet. Then she goes for his face with her nails.

"Sweet Jesus," Sheriff Baxter mutters. "You need help, boy."

He steps between them and pushes Byron toward the cruiser. Sasha follows, still trying to get in as many hits as she can. Sheriff Baxter says she's going to the station too, seeing as she's in possession of stolen merchandise and all. Sasha climbs in beside Byron. We can still hear her shouting even after Sheriff Baxter closes the car door behind her.

"I guess that's that," he says, shaking his head. "Looks like I've got this one all wrapped up."

Great-Aunt Grace isn't going to let him get away with that. "Since y'all were so busy suspectin' me, I had to dig a little deeper than you, Dot, and the other fools," she says loudly. "I had some help, too." She gestures to Tiffany and me.

"Well, good work, I guess," Sheriff Baxter replies, suddenly in a hurry. "I reckon I better get these two down to the station before she kills him."

He doesn't make it a foot away before Great-Aunt Grace calls him back. "Oh, and one more thing, Sheriff."

Sheriff Baxter turns and regards Great-Aunt Grace warily. "I reckon you're looking for an apology?"

"Not at all."

Great-Aunt Grace plucks Eunetta's reward flier from

her stack and holds it up. "Three hundred dollars rewarded to anyone with any information about the pearls' whereabouts. Right there in black and white. I'll take large bills, if you don't mind."

Sheriff Baxter is the very definition of *flabbergasted*. He reaches slowly into his back pocket, takes out his wallet, and pulls out a wad of cash. He drops it into Great-Aunt Grace's outstretched hand. "That's all I've got on me. A hundred and eighty."

Great-Aunt Grace counts the money and places it in her shirt pocket. "That's all right. I'll be by your house later for the rest."

Sheriff Baxter drives off, Sasha still pummeling Byron in the back seat. Great-Aunt Grace shakes her head.

"How'd you know Sasha would be here?" I ask.

"Because Byron Lockett can't breathe unless there's some simple female up underneath him, worshippin' him. Like I said, that fool's got more women than sense."

We start walking away from H&H Auto Service in the heavy Black Lake heat. Tiffany nudges me in the ribs with her elbow. "See? I told you she'd take us on an adventure," she whispers.

Twenty-Six

EVEN though we caught the Black Lake thief today, Great-Aunt Grace is not about to let us miss a few hours of work. We spend the rest of the morning and part of the afternoon at Grace's Goodies. Then around four she closes up, saying, "I reckon news has spread to where it needs to be. It's time to collect."

For the next hour, Great-Aunt Grace makes her way around Black Lake with Tiffany and me in tow, collecting her reward money. She hits up Eunetta first. Eunetta's husband must've told her we were coming, so it takes her forever to answer the door. And when she does, she only opens it wide enough to thrust one hand out, clutching a wad of twenties.

"Pleasure doin' business with you," Great-Aunt Grace tells her.

Eunetta slams the door.

We head to the houses of two other people that Byron

robbed. Sheriff Baxter has promised to retrieve all stolen goods and return them to their rightful owners. Still, no one wants to hand over reward money to Grace Washington for the part she played, least of all Dot, whom we visit last, but Great-Aunt Grace simply points to the bottom of Dot's flier, which reads, *A $100 reward to anyone with any information about my statue.*

By the time we leave Dot standing at her door, steam practically coming out her ears, Great-Aunt Grace has pulled in $550.

~~~~~~

"We could go to Disney World with that," Tiffany says over a dinner of franks and beans.

"Couldn't even pay for a flight," says Great-Aunt Grace.

"I guess," Tiffany concedes. "But when we're living down in Florida, we'll just drive to Disney. Right, Jeanie?"

"Living in Florida?" Great-Aunt Grace asks.

"That's where the perfect place is," Tiffany says around a mouthful of beans. "The place where we're going to go and live when Mommy finds Daddy. Wanna see it?"

Tiffany takes off before Great-Aunt Grace can say no, her bare feet pounding down the hallway and then up the stairs.

"A perfect place, huh?" Great-Aunt Grace asks. I nod, waiting for her to roll her eyes or call us fools for believing there's such a place, but she doesn't. She takes a sip of her water instead.

"So, um, I just wanted to say that, um . . ." I stare down at my plate, as though I might find the words I'm looking for there. "I just wanted to say that I couldn't help but overhear how you stood up to Moon about his smoking. You know, for me."

"Well, don't go gettin' a swelled head about it. That dome of yours is big enough as it is, Lord knows."

A surge of anger pulses through me. "I'm just saying it was cool. That's all. So thanks, okay?"

Silence stretches like an ocean between us. "You're welcome, girl," Great-Aunt Grace says at last. "He'll come around. He acts about your sister's age when he gets mad. Now finish your food before it gets cold."

Tiffany dashes back into the kitchen, brandishing her drawing of the perfect place. She stands beside Great-Aunt Grace and describes each detail to her. The sunlit rooms, her purple bedroom, the smell of cooking food. She's cut off by the sound of the phone ringing.

Great-Aunt Grace goes into the living room to answer it. Tiffany holds up her drawing to the light. "I forgot to color the sky. See?" She shows me the blank, paper-white space hovering above our sky-colored house. From the living room, I hear Great-Aunt Grace say, "Calm down, Lisa. What you mean, you never gonna find him? Listen to me. . . ."

Outside, the evening is quiet and still, but I can feel the earth shift beneath my feet. "I'll be right back," I tell Tiffany.

"Are you on a solo spy mission again?" she asks, still focused on her drawing.

"No. I just need to talk to Great-Aunt Grace for a minute. Stay here."

I walk into the living room just as Great-Aunt Grace hangs up the phone. She's looking down at the floor, her eyebrows scrunched up.

"She's giving up on finding Dad, isn't she?" I ask quietly, standing stock-still, as though disturbing even the air in this room might make the news worse.

Great-Aunt Grace shakes her head. I know she is deciding whether to tell me the truth.

"She's giving up hope?"

Great-Aunt Grace nods. "She told me she don't know where else to look. She followed that credit-card trail, but she thinks he's gone for good this time."

Gone for good this time. I sit heavily on the couch.

"She said she was gettin' close to finding him. So close. That's what she told me."

Great-Aunt Grace and I look up at the same time. I didn't even hear Tiffany come into the room. Tears are in her eyes. She heard every word.

~~~~~~~

Tiffany won't talk. She won't even cry. Great-Aunt Grace paces nervously back and forth across the living room floor. For once, she seems to be at a loss for words.

At last she says, "Guess you two better go on to bed. We'll talk about this in the mornin'."

She tries to hustle us off the couch, but I don't move. Not yet.

"I'll be up in a minute," I say. Great-Aunt Grace takes Tiffany by the wrist and leads her out of the living room.

I head straight for the phone and dial Mr. Brown's number. I know he's not in his office this late. I leave a voicemail anyway, even though he said he'd call me. I tell him that I really, really need him to check our mailbox and if he finds something to call me back ASAP. I hang up the phone and trudge upstairs. Great-Aunt Grace is tucking Tiffany in—the first time she's ever done that. I put on my pajamas and sit down on the edge of my bed. Great-Aunt Grace pats me awkwardly on the shoulder as she leaves, stopping when she gets to the door.

"You want the light on or off?" she asks.

"On." I'm not even close to ready to go to sleep yet.

Great-Aunt Grace nods. Then she's gone. I look over at Tiffany. She is stone.

Why won't she cry? You hear all this stuff on TV about kids who have been through a lot shoving all their feelings into a box deep inside them, locking it, and throwing away the key.

Tiffany catches me looking at her. "Tell me a story," she demands.

"I've got a plan in the works to find Dad. Better than Mom's. You want to hear it?"

"Tell me a story," Tiffany says again.

I make up a story on the spot about two princesses named Tiffany and Jeanie, who live in a purple palace. Tiffany is the more beautiful princess who has the power to turn weeds into cartoon characters.

"And her sister, Princess Jeanie, can travel back and forth through time," I say. "The princesses live happily until one day—"

"Tell it how Daddy would. In the Mickey voice."

I try to do the Mickey Mouse voice, but no one can do it quite like Dad. Tiffany punches the bed, once, twice. Soon she picks up a steady rhythm—*punch, punch, punch*—and a small sound escapes her. Now she starts to cry. Relief floods through me and seeps from my pores. But Tiffany's not stopping. I find Mr. Teddy Daniels curled up in her sheets and run through his skit. I promise her that Mom will find Dad any day now. Nothing works, so I pull her up and out of bed.

Great-Aunt Grace's doorknob is plastic, made to look like crystal. I know better than to turn that sucker without knocking. I tap softly at first, and then harder when she doesn't answer right away. When she finally pulls the door open, it squeals like a newborn.

She doesn't seem surprised to see us, but then, her facial expression doesn't ever change much. "What is it?" she says. A lit cigarette bobs between her lips.

I open my mouth, close it, open it again. I shrug and take a step back. She does the same, letting us in.

Great-Aunt Grace's room doesn't reek of old cigarettes like I expected it to. Her room is cluttered, though, filled with little tables, a sea of canvas bags, and yarn—rolls and rolls of it. Great-Aunt Grace tosses her half-finished ciga-rette out the window and puts on a fan over in the corner. Then she turns to us. She looks nervous, probably because she's never had two kids sitting on her bed before, one crying, the other staring.

She takes something out of one of her many bags. The sea-green baby clothes she'd been working on when Moon came over about the cigarettes. She hands them to Tiffany.

"These are for you. Well, for that teddy bear of yours anyway," she says gruffly. "I'm workin' on a few other out-fits."

Tiffany caresses the overalls and jacket Great-Aunt Grace has made, and sniffles.

Great-Aunt Grace studies us like we're something under a microscope. "Well, I suppose you two are sad about your daddy," Great-Aunt Grace says. "But your mama is just tired of lookin'. It don't mean she's givin' all the way up and it don't mean he won't come on back on his own."

Then she begins to clean her room. Well, not clean it, exactly. She's really just picking things up and putting them back down again. I watch as she pulls a bunch of clothes out of a drawer and puts it on the bed next to me. A few shirts, a pair of pants. And her teeth.

We almost fall off the bed trying to get away from those.

"Shouldn't your teeth be in your mouth?" Tiffany asks.

"Nope. I keep them around so I know that I don't need 'em. I find that the teeth and the spleen are the most over-rated of body parts." Great-Aunt Grace picks up one of the shirts and starts to refold it.

There's a picture on the nightstand, an old, faded photo of a man. It's not Moon. This man is dark brown, wearing a bright orange vest and holding a big gun.

"Who is he?" I ask.

Great-Aunt Grace answers me without looking at the picture. "Someone. I keep his picture so I know I don't need him anymore either."

"Were you guys in looooove?" Tiffany asks.

Great-Aunt Grace looks over at us with her hard black eyes. "I reckon so. But he loved himself more than he ever loved me, so I opened my hands and let him go, long before your time."

I tuck my feet under my butt. "Where is he now?"

Great-Aunt Grace mutters something under her breath that sounds vaguely like "Nosy little things," but aloud she says, "Two hours away with a wife and too many grandkids."

We sit in silence after that. Great-Aunt Grace continues to rearrange her clutter, and every now and then she sneaks a look at us. I know because I'm sneaking looks at her, too. Her face is old and brown and wrinkled, has been since we got here, but her wrinkles look different to me now. They look like little cracks in one of those thousand-year-old buildings, small and unimportant. How do you get as strong as Great-Aunt Grace, strong enough to let go? When I'm not looking at her, I'm looking around her room, half expecting to see a vat of some Courage Potion. But there's nothing in here other than her yarn, pictures, and a bunch of pairs of sneakers with soles so rundown they're almost gone.

The next time I sneak a peek at Great-Aunt Grace, she catches me. And then she does something that just about makes me fall off the bed again. She holds up her teeth and claps them together like they're talking. Tiffany dissolves into a puddle of laughter. I feel a smile spreading across my face. And the more those big yellow teeth clap together, the bigger my smile becomes, until I'm all-out giggling—and I never giggle. Great-Aunt Grace smiles at us, the first time she's ever done that. Her smile is like a baby's, all gums.

Great-Aunt Grace puts the folded clothes back in the

drawer and places her teeth neatly on top of them. Then she goes back to fussing with her things. I wonder if she ever sleeps. Right now I don't feel like sleeping either. I watch as Great-Aunt Grace bends down, wheezing a little, and starts going through her canvas bags. Out falls even more yarn. She's started a few things—a hat, a pair of gloves, a blanket—but nothing is finished. She straightens and points at a ball of yarn on the floor beside me.

"Hand me that, Treasure."

"Why won't you just call me Jeanie?" I ask, sighing as I hand the yarn over.

"Jeanie's not your name."

"It's *part* of my name. Besides, I don't like my name anymore. Treasure Jeanie May Daniels. Flops around in your mouth like a dying fish."

Great-Aunt Grace throws her head back and laughs that great big booming laugh of hers. I jump. "Dyin'?" she says. "I don't think so. There's life in it yet."

She starts organizing her yarn creations, and I reach over and pluck the photo from the nightstand. What was he like? Does Great-Aunt Grace still miss him? The man in the picture has a mustache that reminds me of Daddy's.

"Do you think Dad loves himself more than he loves us?" I blurt out.

For the first time since we've entered her room, Great-Aunt Grace stops moving. "Of course not, girl. He's just lost, is all."

I put the picture down on the bed next to me and pull my feet out from under me. "Most of the time we feel lost too," I say.

"How so?" Great-Aunt Grace says. "Tell me."

And we do. We tell her everything, the words pouring out of us the way rain plummets from the sky. Tiffany tells her how we'd come home from school to find our stuff packed up and ready to go, and Dad downstairs already warming up the car. I tell her how it feels like we've been running behind him for years, but we don't ever know where we're headed or how long we'll stay.

"It's a travesty," I say.

Great-Aunt Grace cocks her head to the side. "You know a lot of million-dollar words, huh? You're gonna have to teach me some."

"I'm always leaving my friends," Tiffany adds. "It's a travesty too." Tiffany pauses. "A travesty is bad, right, Jeanie?"

"Yes, and friends are overrated."

"What you call Terrance, then?" Great-Aunt Grace asks. "I seen him walkin' you to my store."

"We're associates."

"Associates?"

I nod. "No sense in making friends if we're going to move anyway. I never told Dad this, but sometimes I hate moving. I just want to stay in one place long enough to catch my breath."

Great-Aunt Grace nods like she understands. If some-one had told me I'd be sitting here like this with her, pour-ing out my heart, I would've laughed until I had an asthma attack.

Tiffany holds up Mr. Teddy Daniels's new outfit and studies it. "You need a new name," she says to Great-Aunt Grace.

"What you mean, girl? My name is Grace."

"I mean a new *other* name besides the one Jeanie some-times calls you." I reach over and try to pinch Tiffany. She swats my hand away.

"What you been callin' me, girl?"

"Um," I say.

"Sometimes Jeanie calls you Gag," Tiffany replies mat-ter-of-factly.

"Gag?" Great-Aunt Grace looks to me for an explana-tion.

"It's the initials for Great-Aunt Grace, but you know, like, in a bad way. Like, *Gag me,* or whatever."

I wait for Great-Aunt Grace to kick me out of her room. She stares at me, her face expressionless. Then she bursts out laughing again. "Lord knows I've been called worse." She reaches beneath her nightstand and comes up with a jumbo-size bag of Hershey's Kisses. She pops two in her mouth, bites right into them, and then pops in two more. She's right. You don't need teeth.

"So, what should we call you?" Tiffany wonders aloud,

tapping her chin with her index finger. "What about Auntie?"

"You two can call me any old thing you like. Here, have these."

Auntie scoops up a handful of Hershey's Kisses and dumps them on the bed in front of us. I drop the photo and scramble to catch them before they roll off. Auntie sits down on the bed and that's us for a while, me and Tiffany chewing, her gumming. Tiffany moves over so Auntie can sit between us, her bare arms touching mine and Tiffany's. Her skin is darker than the candy, and together we look like swirls of caramel and milk chocolate.

"Your skin is very black," Tiffany says.

"Born black," Auntie says. She rises from the bed and leaves the room, her nightgown thrown over her arm. When she returns, she's all decked out for bed in a floral nightie that comes down to just above her ankles. She reaches over and pulls the blankets back for us. She fluffs up the pillows, too, before climbing in beside us, the bed sinking beneath her weight. "Now sleep," she says.

We sleep. And wake up with silver wrappers in our hair.

Twenty-Seven

WHEN I wake up the next morning, the sun is warm on my face. Auntie is already up and gone, her blinds pulled open and her bedroom door cracked. I stretch my legs, and my feet brush up against something soft and sharp all at once. I sit up fast and pull my feet back before Mr. Shuffle can sink another claw into my big toe.

"You're so fat and evil."

He blinks big moon-colored eyes and flicks his tail like a middle finger.

Tiffany squirms in her sleep. Her eyes are puffy from crying, and there is drool on her cheek.

"Is Mommy back yet? Did she find Daddy?" she asks, her eyes still closed.

"No."

Tiffany whimpers. I take her hand, pull her out of bed, and lead her downstairs. The smell of frying bacon meets us halfway to the kitchen. Auntie stands at the stove, her back to us. I push Tiffany into a chair at the table and Auntie says gruffly, "Is that Tiffany cryin' again?"

"I . . . want . . . Mommy . . . and Daddy!" Tiffany howls.

I'm sure that wherever Mommy is, she can hear Tiffany loud and clear.

Auntie turns around to look at us, her face all business. "Let's go," she says in the same hard voice.

She sounds like Gag again. I hesitate. "Go?" I ask.

"Yes, girl," she answers. "Now, come on and quit askin' questions."

Auntie turns to leave. Tiffany and I exchange a startled look and jump up to follow her, barefoot and wearing only our pajamas. Auntie goes straight out the back door and down the stairs.

"You comin' or not?"

I take Tiffany's hand and pull her gently outside, wondering just what the heck Auntie is up to. Yesterday, when she was still Great-Aunt Grace, I would have thought she was taking us out back to feed us to something big, hairy, and southern. But now, I get the feeling things are different. I look over at Tiffany as we stand on the top step. The only reason she isn't crying anymore is because she's too busy being confused.

I sure hope Auntie knows what she's doing.

We go down the steps and over to Auntie, who is standing under a tree.

"Reach down and touch the ground," she instructs.

"Seriously?" I ask.

Auntie nods. What in the world this has to do with Tiffany missing Mom and Dad, I don't know. Unless, of course, Auntie's plan is to distract Tiffany. If so, it's working. Tiffany bends down and runs her hands over the ground in front of us. I do the same, the grass tickling my palms, until my hand stops on something hard and cold. Stone.

"Girls, I'd like you to meet your great-grandmother and grandfather."

Tiffany jumps back. "They're here, in the ground?" she asks, her voice shaky.

"Yes, but you don't need to be afraid. My mama and daddy were good strong people who wouldn't hurt a fly. Unless that fly talked back. Then they'd warm its buns." Auntie laughs, and I wonder how getting spanked could ever be funny. When Auntie speaks again, her voice is soft and low. "Whenever I get to missin' the two of them, I just come out here and strike up a conversation."

"You mean, like, with their ghosts?" Tiffany asks, inching closer to me.

"No such thing as ghosts. I talk to their essence, their spirits."

Sounds like ghosts to me. But I'm supposed to be acting brave, for Tiffany's sake, of course.

"Did you say you miss your parents sometimes?" Tiffany asks. *"You?"*

Auntie laughs. "I'm not made of stone, girl. Of course I miss my mama and daddy. Everyone does. And there ain't nothin' wrong with it."

"But once you start missing them, how do you stop?"

"You don't."

I can almost hear Tiffany's face fall.

"You just need something, is all. Something of your mama and daddy's you can keep near to you. Come on in. I think I got just the thing."

Once inside, Auntie goes into the living room and flips on the light. She takes a big book from one of the shelves and blows the dust off it. A photo album. Tiffany and I watch wordlessly as she flips through it, her eyebrows bent in concentration. Finally, she pulls out a photo, a real old one with a black, shiny backing, and hands it to Tiffany face-down. Tiffany turns it over. It's a picture of Mom and Dad from years ago at what appears to be a barbecue, Dad's arm slung over Mom's shoulder. They're smiling, Dad widest of all. Tiffany takes the picture and hugs it to her chest.

A lump forms in my throat. What if this picture is one of the only things we have left of Dad? What if he never comes back?

My mouth won't ask the question, but my face must do the talking because Auntie looks me in the eye and says, "Your daddy ain't gone for good. Your mama may not find him, but I reckon he'll come back on his own. No man in his right mind would leave the two of you, even though y'all are spoiled as the day is long. I promise you that."

At that moment, I would have believed Auntie if she'd told us grass was blue and the sky green.

"Jane told me losing hope is kind of like losing the will to live," I say.

"Jane is a fool, and she's wrong as snow in August for half of the outfits she wears, but I reckon she may be right about that."

Auntie goes back into the kitchen then to finish cooking breakfast. We eat burnt bacon and dry eggs, hope hovering above us like a fog.

~~~~~

After breakfast is over and I've done the dishes, we sit around the table for a bit, working on Auntie's word find, nobody seemingly in a hurry to get over to Grace's Goodies.

"Let's just not go to work," I suggest.

"And who's gonna pay my bills?" Auntie asks. She runs her index finger over the jumbled letters of her word find, searching for one. "Sinister," she mutters.

"It means really evil, like the devil-evil," I say.

"Or like Jaguar," Tiffany adds.

"I see." Great-Aunt Grace finds *sinister* and draws a large, loopy oval around it. "You know, you never told me what Jaguar said to y'all that made Treasure lose her ever-lovin' mind."

"What she said to me—Jeanie—was that I'm a loser whose parents don't want her."

"Is that right?" Auntie says calmly.

"It is," Tiffany says. "And then she banged up your store, too."

"She sure enough did. Speakin' of the store . . ."

"Let's not go," I say again. "I'll die if I have to clean another shelf."

"Is it really that bad, girl?"

I nod, and Auntie nods too. I can see the gears whirring in her mind. "Tiffany, go put some shoes on. Treasure, go do your hair. We got thangs to do."

"I already did my hair."

"Well, go on upstairs and try again. I got a chain saw out back in my shed if you need it."

Auntie is a real comedian. I trudge back to the bathroom and to Auntie's hard-bristle brush and Blue Magic grease. Then I get to slicking and brushing until I get a decent half-ponytail, half-bun going. Tiffany puts on her sandals, and we meet Auntie at the front door. She looks at my hair and shakes her head. "Lord, have mercy," she mutters.

Auntie locks up, and before we know it, we're trucking up Iron Horse Road. We stop at Grace's Goodies and I try to mentally prepare myself for the shelves, but Auntie says we're not staying. She grabs one of the videotapes Tiffany labeled and a package each of Sour Patch Kids for Tiffany and me.

"To keep y'all from whinin'. We got a walk ahead of us."

"What's she up to?" I ask, my eyes on Auntie's broad back as she marches up Main Street with us trailing behind.

"We're going on another adventure," Tiffany says. She tears into her pack of Sour Patch Kids and eats them two at a time.

Auntie said we had a walk ahead of us. She should've used the word *trek*, as in a long, hot, awful journey. I gobble down my Sour Patch Kids as we pound the pavement until we're all dripping with sweat and dying of thirst. Until we come at last to a tree-lined street and stop in front of a white brick house with a wraparound porch and shutters that match the front door. The lawn looks like some guy from the army gave it a military-issue crewcut. Even the flowers in the garden stand at attention. This is the kind of house that probably has an alarm system and guard dogs, but Auntie doesn't hesitate before striding up the walkway.

"Y'all come on," she calls to us. She rings the bell.

"Who lives here?" I ask, hanging back, Tiffany's sticky hand in mine.

No answer, from Auntie or from inside the house. It's not even nine in the morning on a weekday, too early for visiting, but here we are. Auntie rings the bell again. This time we hear footsteps on the other side of the door.

The door opens, and there stands Jaguar. She stares at us, open-mouthed, a flimsy screen the only thing separating her from the mighty Grace Washington.

"Wh-what are you doing here?"

"I'm here to collect, for the damage you did to my store. Now step aside, girl, and let me in."

Twenty-Eight

J AGUAR, who's that at the door?"

Jaguar's father, Pastor Burroughs, appears behind her. He's wearing a bathrobe and slippers, and when he sees Auntie, he adds a scowl to his outfit.

"Ms. Washington, do you have any idea what time it is?"

"I sure enough do. It's time for your daughter to pay."

"Pay for what?"

"For comin' into my store and messin' it up last Sunday."

"Jaguar would never do such a thing."

"I got a tape that says otherwise."

Jaguar sucks in her breath. So does Pastor Burroughs. So do I. What Auntie's got is a blank tape, and if Pastor Burroughs finds out, we'll be in a world of trouble.

Auntie looks around both father and daughter and into the house. "Now y'all gonna let me in or what? I'm fryin' up like chicken out here, Lord knows I am."

Wordlessly, Jaguar and her father step aside. Auntie beckons to Tiffany and me to follow. No one invites us to sit down in the living room, but Auntie takes a seat on the long white couch anyway. The Burroughses' living room is the cleanest place I've ever seen—and I've been in a few hospitals. The first floor is open and airy, and everything is beige—the tile in the entryway, the area rugs, and the couches. It's straight out of a home decorating magazine.

"Jaguar, who on earth is here?" a woman's voice calls from upstairs.

"Ms. Washington," Jaguar answers.

Mrs. Burroughs is down the stairs in a flash, dressed for work but with her hair still done up in pink rollers.

"Good morning, Charlene," Auntie says, smiling and nodding. "Why don't the three of you have a seat?" She gestures to the couch across from ours, inviting the Burroughses to sit down in their own house.

Mrs. Burroughs nudges Jaguar, who slinks over and sits down across from us. Her mother joins her. Pastor Burroughs stays on his feet.

"Now, I don't believe all of you have met my grand-nieces from up north."

Pastor Burroughs narrows his eyes. "Is that what all this is about?" he demands to know.

"All *what* is about?" says Mrs. Burroughs.

"That girl there"—he points at me—"is the one who attacked Jaguar at camp, and now Ms. Washington is here talking nonsense. What is this? Blackmail? Extortion?" Pastor Burroughs is gearing up for full-on preaching mode.

Jaguar's mother looks lost. Jaguar looks at the floor.

"It ain't blackmail or extortion. I'm here for one thing and one thing only: to right a wrong. Your daughter came into my store and wrecked my shelves, knockin' candy all over the place."

The room goes quiet. "Prove it," Mrs. Burroughs says.

Auntie holds up her tape. Her blank tape. I swallow hard. Auntie points at the label with last Sunday's date, written in Tiffany's shaky, seven-year-old handwriting. "You got a VCR?" she asks.

They do. Mrs. Burroughs pulls open the doors of their entertainment unit. She holds out her hand for the tape. Auntie hands it to her, but just as Mrs. Burroughs reaches for it, Auntie snatches it back.

"Are you sure you want to watch this? Do you really want to bear witness to Jungle Cat here—"

"Jaguar," Pastor Burroughs cuts in.

"My apologies. Do you really want to bear witness to Jaguar destroyin' an old woman's property? She is your baby girl, after all, isn't she?" Auntie clears her throat. "My, my, I sure could use a glass of water with a slice of lemon," she says.

No one moves.

"I want to see the tape," Pastor Burroughs spits out.

"Are you sure?" Auntie asks. "Can your heart take it, Pastor, watchin' your daughter behave like a hooligan?" She turns to Jaguar. "Why not spare your parents, girl, and tell them every drop of the truth."

Jaguar looks down at her clenched hands. Her knuckles have gone white.

"The tape, Ms. Washington. I want to see it now."

"No!" Jaguar shouts, jumping up. "I did mess up her store that day." She locks eyes with Auntie. "And I'm really, really sorry about it, okay?"

"No, ma'am, it's not. You gonna pay your debt to me."

"What do you want?" Mrs. Burroughs asks, fear creeping into her voice.

"Firstly, I'll be needing a pitcher of water for me and my grandnieces to wet our whistle. Don't let a slice of lemon or two kill you."

Mrs. Burroughs sends Jaguar into the kitchen to fetch a pitcher of ice water—she doesn't tell her to add lemon—and three glasses. Auntie doesn't say another word until her whistle is wet.

"So is it money you want?" Pastor Burroughs asks. "Because we can pay for any merchandise Jaguar damaged, but we expect you to be, um . . . discreet about all this."

Auntie looks to me. "Discreet?"

"He means he wants you to keep Jaguar's nasty ways on the down low so as not to tarnish his outstanding reputation."

Pastor Burroughs fixes me with a hot glare, while Auntie takes another long and thoughtful sip of water. "I'll agree to be discreet, as you say, but it ain't money I want. It's time."

"Time?" says Jaguar.

"Yes, time, girl. You see, my grandniece here is real good and tired of cleanin' shelves at my store, so I'm gonna be needin' someone to relieve her of this duty. I reckon you'll be a right good fit for the job."

Jaguar shakes her head. "You can't make me clean shelves. Mommy, Daddy, do something!"

"There's nothing can be done," Auntie says. "This discreetness your daddy is after comes at a price, girl, unless of course that price is too high for y'all to pay . . . "

"It's not," Mrs. Burroughs says quickly. Pastor Burroughs doesn't say a word. He can't take his eyes off of Auntie, even as she stands and indicates that Tiffany and I should do the same.

"Lovely seeing all of you," she says, waving gaily and setting her empty glass down. I've never seen her so close to cheerful. "We ought to do this more often." And to Jaguar, she adds, "I'll let you know when I'm ready for you to get to work, girl, and don't you dare think about not showin' up."

We let ourselves out.

Twenty-Nine

MR. Brown said he would call me by today but I don't want to wait. We've only just gotten from Jaguar's house to Goodies—it's a little after nine—so I'll give Mr. Brown some time to get settled in at his desk before I call. I go out to the front and sit behind the counter with Auntie and Tiffany, and we pick up where we left off on the walk over here, laughing about Jaguar and the shelves and Byron and all his women. Auntie lets us have free candy today, though she tells us not to go expecting it all the time.

Yesterday evening, when we got back from Grace's Goodies, Auntie did what she calls cleaning. "Can't have Ms. Drama over here, havin' another asthma attack," she said. She mostly just dusted some things and moved other things around. Her clutter remained everywhere and on top of everything. Books, magazines, figurines. She must've lived at 9 Iron Horse Road forever to fill those rooms up the way she has. Most of the places we've lived were so bare and empty of pictures and knickknacks, you'd never know that four people were staying there. They weren't homes like Auntie's, but pit stops on a journey that never seems to end. I close my eyes and imagine the odd smell of Auntie's house with its mixture of spicy, smoky, and sweet. It's warm and familiar.

My eyes snap open. Moving Rule Number Four: *Don't get attached to the place.*

I slide off the stool between Auntie and Tiffany and go back to the stockroom. I pick up the phone and hold it until it starts barking that off-the-hook sound at me. I put it back, then pick it up again and dial. Mr. Brown's secretary answers and places me on hold.

Then Mr. Brown says, "Right on time, kid."

"Yeah."

"Good thing you called. I'm about to leave for a week in the Poconos with my old lady." Mr. Brown pauses.

"That sounds nice," I say.

"To you, yeah, but that's because you don't know my wife. Anyway, I checked the mail yesterday and found a letter from your father in your box. What you want me to do with it, kid? You want me to read it to you? Give you the return address? What?"

My hands are shaking. I can scarcely breathe.

"Hey, kid, you there? I don't have all—"

"Read it to me, please, and tell me the return address."

Mr. Brown sighs. I hear him rip the envelope open. "It says, 'I'm sorry. I love you all.' Seriously? Is that it?"

"What's the return address?" I ask, my voice trembling.

"Sixteen forty-one Brewer Street, Cranford, North Carolina. You got that, kid?"

I repeat the address in my head again and again. "Yes, I got it."

"Good." He pauses. "I hope everything works out for you," he says, and hangs up.

I sit down on the cold stockroom floor. Dad wrote to us. Six words. He's been gone almost three months and he wrote us six words. But we have an address now. We can go there and—

"Girl, what you doin' down on the floor?"

I look up to find Auntie peering at me from the doorway.

"I know where Dad is," I say, and my voice sounds strange. Flat. Joyless. Not excited, the way I imagined it would when I found out something—anything—about Dad.

"Is that right?" Auntie says softly. "Where's he at?"

I recite the address in the same flat voice.

"So he's still in North Carolina, then," Auntie says. "Guess you'd better call your mama and tell her."

"Right now?" I ask.

Auntie nods. She takes the phone off the hook and holds it out to me.

I climb to my feet and take it from her. She waits until

I dial Mom's number before she walks away. Jane said happiness doesn't come easy, and she's right.

Mom answers the phone. "I still can't find him," she says, before I even say hello. Her voice breaks. "I even drove all the way back to Delaware last night. No trace of him. What are we going to do now?"

We could stay here in Black Lake, I say in my mind.

Mom sucks in her breath, and I realize that she's crying. "He can't just leave us like this. We need him. I need him."

Guilt fills up every inch of me. Jane said happiness is about making sacrifices. "I know where Dad is."

Mom sniffles. "What? How?"

I tell her all about my phone call to Mr. Brown and about the letter and the return address.

"Christ, I can't believe Mr. Brown gave you any information at all, with his evil self. What did the letter say?"

"'I'm sorry. I love you all.'"

Mom's silent for a long time. "The important thing is that we know where he is."

"And what are going to do when he's standing in front of us?" I ask.

"We're gonna make him come back. Then we lay down the law. Tell him he can't ever do this again. We'll find a new place to live, a permanent place, and —"

And what if it doesn't work? What if he runs away again or we have to keep moving from place to place?

"I don't understand why you don't sound happy about this," Mom says suddenly. "You told us all to keep having hope, and we did, and now we found him."

I shake my questions from my head. We found Dad. Together we're going to go get him and bring him back and then we will be an aggregate again.

"I am happy," I say, forcing my voice up an octave.

"Good. I'll be there tomorrow afternoon. Do me a favor and put your sister on the phone."

I call Tiffany from the front of the store, where she's interrogating Auntie about why she doesn't sell sour-punch straws. Tiffany delivers the excitement Mom is looking for. She screams and shrieks and carries on when Mom tells her how soon she'll be here to get us, and when she hangs up the phone, she runs back out to the front of the store. I follow slowly and watch as Tiffany climbs into the stool beside Auntie and engulfs her in a hug.

"We're going to the perfect place," she says.

"I hope so," Auntie says.

"Are you gonna miss us?" Tiffany asks her, resting her head on Auntie's shoulder.

"You mean your cryin' and your sister's talkin' back? Not one bit. Like I told you, I ain't one for company."

Auntie nudges Tiffany off of her and goes around the counter to straighten the racks of candy. Tiffany comes over to where I'm standing in the entrance to the stock-room and slips her arm around my waist.

"I think I'll miss Auntie," she says. "Even if she won't miss us."

"Yeah. Me too."

Tiffany returns to her stool and proceeds to spin around and around on it like a maniac. I go back into the stockroom and sit down on the floor, pretending I can see the future like Jane. But what I see is in the past: eating Hershey's Kisses with Auntie, walking home from Camp Jesus Saves with Terrance.

"You all right, girl?"

I open my eyes at the sound of Auntie's voice.

"Yeah."

"Good." She points to a middle shelf across from me. "Out of Kit Kats," she mutters, not meeting my eyes.

When she leaves and I'm alone in the stockroom again, I get up and start scrubbing shelves. I scrub until my shoulders are sore, trying to erase the idea of staying in Black Lake. That's not what the future holds.

Thirty

THE doorbell rings the next morning. Terrance is standing on the other side of the screen door, nervously rocking his weight from foot to foot.

"Hi."

"Hi."

We stand there, looking at everything but each other, until he says, "Can I come in?"

"It's 'May I,' and yes."

Terrance's face breaks into a smile as he steps inside. "You haven't changed a bit." He joins me in Auntie's living room, where he stops and looks at her furnishings. "So," he says, his eyes on her antique clock, "I haven't seen you around camp lately. Did Ms. Eunetta suspend you?"

"No. I'm just not going back."

"That's too bad," Terrance says. He starts walking around and ends up in the kitchen. I'm right behind him. He jumps, as though he's startled to see Auntie in her own house, putting the orange juice back in the fridge. "Good morning, Ms. Washington."

"Mornin', Terrance," Auntie replies, not turning around. "You eat?"

"Yes. I had three Pop-Tarts before I left my grandmother's house."

Terrance still has the crumbs on his shirt and in the corner of his mouth to prove it. Auntie turns to where Tiffany is plopped at the kitchen table and says, "Come on outside with me. I want to show you something in the back."

"All you have in the back is dead people," Tiffany whines.

"Girl, just come on," Auntie snaps.

Tiffany hops to her feet, and the two of them hurry out the back door, leaving me alone with Terrance. He goes over to the kitchen window and peeks outside.

"You know, I heard you guys caught the thief."

"You heard right."

"Serves Byron right. Seriously, how many girlfriends does one guy need?"

"At least three, apparently."

I tell Terrance all about our trip to Jaguar's house yesterday, and how she's going to have to clean the shelves at Grace's Goodies on account of her wrecking Auntie's store.

"Dang," Terrance says. "Cleaning those shelves is rough."

"Yeah, I kind of feel bad for her," I say.

"Really?"

"No. I was just being facetious." Terrance stares at me blankly. "It means I was joking."

"You're gonna have to write that word down for me too."

"Sure."

"Cool. I should get going. I just stopped by to see if you were coming back to camp," Terrance says. He heads for the front door, then stops suddenly, his hand hovering above the door handle. "Do you want to hang out after church tomorrow?"

"Um . . ."

"As, like, associates."

I won't be here tomorrow. "What about today? Right now?"

Terrance's eyes go wide. "O-kay, I guess. If it's all right with Ms. Washington."

I go out back to ask her. She and Tiffany are looking up at something in the tree above Auntie's parents' graves.

"It's not a nest," Tiffany is saying.

"It is, girl. Use your eyes," Auntie replies impatiently.

I clear my throat to get Auntie's attention. When I have it, I ask if it would be all right if I hung out with Terrance for a while.

"I reckon so. We'll just be hangin' around here, waitin' on your mama."

Ever since Mom called last night, I've been checking for signs that Auntie cares about us leaving, that she'll miss us even a tiny bit. I don't see anything. But then her face doesn't ever change much.

Terrance is waiting for me at the edge of Auntie's lawn.

"Do you mind if we go for a walk?" I ask him. "A short one."

"Okay. Cool. Where do you want to go?"

I reach into my pocket and finger the last of the emergency money Mom gave me. The sun is butter-yellow and scorching. "All over." I think of Auntie. "I've got *thangs* to do."

"Seriously?"

"Yes."

We stop at Jane's first. The restaurant is a mess of plastic tables and chairs and gauzy curtains. She is wiping down the counter when we enter. "Well, well, what brings you here today, little miss?" she says, straightening. She eyes Terrance. "And you are . . . ?"

"Terrance Gall. I moved here a few months ago from Mississippi."

"I see. You plan on being some kind of scientist one day, huh?"

"I do." Terrance shuffles from foot to foot. "Was that a prediction?"

"You'd better hope not, 'cause predictions cost five dollars. Speaking of which . . ." Jane's eyes find me. Her lids are coated in purple and gold eye shadow. I pull the money out of my pocket before she can blink. She stuffs it in her ample cleavage, where it disappears completely. Terrance stares, mesmerized.

"Well, thanks for telling me my future," I say.

"You're welcome." We turn to go. "Tell me, girl, did you find that happiness yet?"

I think about staying up and eating Hershey's Kisses with Auntie, about her demanding that Jaguar clean the shelves at Grace's Goodies, about sharing words with Terrance. But what I'm feeling is guilt. Thinking about being together with Dad again should be making me happy, but it's not.

"No. Not yet," I say.

"Well, it's coming soon, girl, so don't stop waiting on it."

The door chimes as we leave.

"Where to next?" Terrance asks.

"What about the lake?"

"It's more of a reservoir, but okay."

As we walk, Terrance fills me in on what I've missed at camp. Jaguar and Pamela haven't bothered him too much lately. In fact, he's not sure the two of them are even speaking to each other these days.

We come to the woods and slip through the opening in the trees. "What happened?" I ask.

"Who knows? Girls are weird. No offense."

"None taken."

We walk silently through the woods, and it's just as peaceful and beautiful as I remember, and the lake just as gross. We stand on the shore and watch the waves push the algae around until I catch sight of a figure a little farther along, tossing stones in the water.

"Is that . . . ?"

"Pamela," Terrance confirms.

We exchange a look. "Let's pretend we didn't see her," Terrance says.

But Pamela has seen us, and she starts over. She stops a ways away, a plastic bag dangling from her hand. I'm sure by now she's heard all about Jaguar getting into trouble, and maybe she wants to have words about it.

"What do you want?" I call out.

"Just wanted to—" Pamela hesitates. "Y'all skipping stones again?"

"No, just looking at the water." I pause, choosing my next words carefully. "Why? You feel like skipping some?"

Pamela takes a step forward and then another until she's standing an arm's length away. She shrugs. "I wouldn't mind, except I don't know how." She glances at Terrance. "Can you show me?"

"Um," Terrance says.

"Yes, he can." I give him a nudge. "Show. Her."

Terrance goes in search of stones for Pamela to skip.

She and I stand in silence as he does, sneaking looks at each other every now and again.

When it's time for Terrance to begin his lesson, he stands as far away from Pamela as he can. She hardly seems to notice, or maybe she doesn't care. She puts down her plastic bag and picks up on stone-skipping after just a few tries.

"Okay, so I get two wishes?" she asks after a pretty successful skip.

Terrance and I nod. Pamela shuts her eyes tight. I notice that she's not wearing her glittery eye shadow or tinted lip-gloss today. She opens her eyes and kicks at the ground, rustling her bag in the process.

"Cookies. For my mama. She's not doing too well."

I remember the frail woman at church wrapped up in blankets and scarves.

"I'm sorry to hear that," Terrance says.

Pamela nods her thanks. "You know, you two don't suck," she says.

"Um, thanks, I guess," I reply.

Pamela takes a stone from the pile at her feet. "I didn't mean it like that. It's just—I guess what I'm trying to say is, my bad. I let Jag get in my head all the time." Pamela tosses the stone from hand to hand. "She's messing up my karma, real talk."

Pamela falls silent again as she goes back to skipping

stones. She works her way through her pile and then bends down to pick up her bag. I wonder how many of her wishes had to do with helping her mom feel better.

"I'll see you guys," she says. She turns to go, and then stops. "And I hope whatever y'all are wishing for comes true," she adds, and hurries off without looking back.

"I told you girls are weird," Terrance says, staring after Pamela. He shakes his head. "Hey, look what I found."

He thrusts his hand in his pocket and whips it out fast, pulling out squares of paper in the process. They drift lazily downward before the breeze catches them and sweeps them away. I recognize my own handwriting at once, words I've given Terrance. He manages to snatch up *melancholy* (*a prolonged and gloomy state of mind—think Ms. Washington*) and I grab *acquiescence* (*agreeing in silence; giving in without a fight, like a sucker*), but it is too late for the rest. They've already glided out into the water.

"Dang it!" Terrance watches the papers float away. "Will you write them down for me again tomorrow?"

Tomorrow I won't be here.

"Sure."

"Thanks. Here." Terrance hands me what he meant to pull out of his pocket in the first place, a stone. It's grayish-black and oblong. "I found it while I was getting stones for Pamela. Look at the contours and the aerodynamics. It'll skip four times at least, for sure. Try it."

I take the stone from Terrance. It is still warm from his hand. Wishes well up inside me.

I wish I could stay here.

I wish that when we find Dad, we stay in the same place forever.

I wish I could be with Auntie and Terrance.

I wish I were home.

The wishes collide and cancel each other out until I'm left with nothing but the weight of the stone in the center of my palm. I place the stone in my pocket. "I think I'll save it." I look up at the sky. Mom will be here soon. "We should go."

~~~~~~~~

We beat a path back the way we came, all the way to Auntie's house.

"You didn't have to walk me here," I say.

He shrugs. "I'm a gentleman. Hey, you want to hang out again tomorrow?"

"Sure."

He doesn't know that I'll be gone before the day is out, that I'm not even going to say goodbye. It's easier this way, for both of us.

"Okay, cool," Terrance says.

I watch him walk away. "Thanks for the stone," I call out.

"No problem," he calls back, and then, for some reason,

he takes off running. He's got an all-over-the-place run, like a puppy. When he's halfway up Iron Horse Road, he turns back and waves. I pretend not to see. Terrance is the kind of kid someone might be stupid enough to miss.

Soon he's a blur in the distance. I look away so I don't have to watch him disappear completely.

Thirty-One

WHEN I get back to Auntie's house, she tells me to go upstairs and get everything packed and by the front door. Tiffany claims she's helping, carrying only her Disney Fund and Mr. Teddy D. I have to make two trips with the suitcases and my asthma machine. When we're done, Auntie makes us peanut-butter sandwiches and pours orange juice, and the three of us sit down at the table and eat.

"So are you gonna order sour-punch straws for the store or not?" Tiffany asks Auntie.

"Maybe," Auntie replies.

"I think they'll really help your business, because they're delicious. One time I ate so many I burned a hole in my tongue."

"It wasn't a hole, silly," I say.

"It was." Tiffany rolls her eyes at me. "Big as a quarter, that hole was."

Auntie is watching Tiffany. Then she blinks, as though

coming out of a trance. "You put every last drop of your stuff by the front door, girl?" I nod. "Good. I don't want to have to be parcel-postin' y'all stuff two months from now."

"You won't," I assure her. "By the way, when is Jaguar coming to clean the shelves?"

"I was thinkin' maybe next week sometime."

"She shouldn't have messed with your store," I say, smiling at the thought of Jaguar's fancy clothes covered in pine-scented cleaner.

"No," Auntie says. "She shouldn't have messed with the two of you."

My breath catches in my throat. "You did all that because of us?"

"Don't go gettin'—"

"A swelled head about it, I know: My dome is big enough as it is."

"You got that right."

The doorbell rings. Auntie gets to her feet.

"That'll be your mama." Tiffany jumps up.

"Well, don't just sit there, gawpin'," Auntie says to me. "Get up off your butt, girl, and let's go."

We meet Mom at the front door. She looks exhausted, but there's a smile on her face as she throws her arms around each of us in turn. Auntie offers to make her a peanut-butter sandwich, but Mom is ready to hit the road.

"Hang on a minute," Auntie says, digging around in her pants pocket. She pulls out a wad of cash and hands it to

Mom. "Five hundred and fifty dollars toward startin' over. Spend it wisely, 'cause Lord knows it didn't come easy."

I stare as Auntie hands the money over to Mom.

"What, you thought I'd keep it to make up for all the food y'all ate?" Auntie says. I nod.

"Well, you thought wrong."

"Thank you," Mom says, pocketing the cash. "For everything. I'll mail you a check as soon as we're settled."

"From you, I'm gonna need cash or a money order," Auntie replies.

Mom says, "Grace, you nut," and slaps at Auntie's arm, but I don't think Auntie was joking.

"Did they behave?" Mom asks.

"Mostly," Auntie answers, with a hint of a smile.

We start carrying our bags outside. It doesn't take long to load up the truck.

"Say goodbye and thank you to your great-aunt," Mom instructs us.

Auntie is standing on her front steps. Tiffany runs up to her and throws her arms around Auntie's middle. Auntie pats her back awkwardly. She's not much for company, and she's not much for hugging, either.

"Don't forget the sour-punch straws," Tiffany yells over her shoulder as she runs to the truck.

Now it's my turn to say goodbye. I walk over to the stairs and hold up my hands, palm out. "Don't worry. I'm not going to hug you."

Auntie laughs.

Mom turns on the ignition and guns the engine. In just a few short minutes, the three of us will be shooting down the interstate toward Cranford, North Carolina. But what if Dad isn't there? What if he is? Panic wells up inside me.

"I'm not sure I want to go," I blurt out.

"But you have to," Auntie says.

"Will you at least miss us?"

"Every day."

Auntie turns her face from mine. I know she's trying to make herself steel again. Make it so it doesn't hurt to have to say goodbye. I know because I've been doing it my whole life.

"I wish we could stay here," I say. Six words, skipping over the waves of Black Lake.

"But you can't, because y'all don't listen," she says.

"You don't clean."

"You got a smart mouth."

"You can't cook."

"You talk back."

"I kind of like you," I say.

"I kind of like you, too," Auntie says. "Now, go on, git."

Thirty-Two

WE have an address: 1641 Brewer Street, Cranford, North Carolina. Mom has the map spread out across my lap. "Cranford is there," she says, pointing.

"We'll take Route 29 till we get to the North Carolina border," she murmurs, more to herself than to me, as she pulls out onto the highway. "Should take us a little over three hours."

Tiffany is bouncing around in the back seat. Mom taps out a steady rhythm on the steering wheel.

"Why didn't he call instead of writing?" I ask.

"Because he knew I'd curse him out," Mom says, jerking the car into the center lane.

We drive and drive. The sun is beginning to go down. The sky has gone from brilliant blue to the color of faded denim on the horizon. We still have an hour to go. My eyes try to close, but I won't let them. Mom turns up the radio and I sing along, just to stay awake.

She pulls off at an exit on the right. We drive on a smaller highway for a bit, and then a narrow two-way street. I stare out the window, unblinking. From either side of the street, small, lopsided houses stare back at me, their glass eyes lit dimly from inside. What would make Dad come to a place like this? Maybe Brewer Street is nicer. I make a note of each street we pass: Cedar, Pine, Everlet. Fields and trees. Mom's neck is damp with sweat.

"Are we lost?"

"I think I missed a turn or something," Mom mutters.

We go back the way we came and find only more fields and trees. No Brewer Street. Mom pulls into a gas station. "Brewer Street?" she calls out to the attendant.

He tells us which way to go. A right puts us on First Street. We drive slowly past houses until we come to another stoplight.

"The street should be coming up on our left," Mom says.

My skin prickles. Tiffany is leaning all the way forward, her face practically in the front seat. Mom turns onto Brewer Street. My heart climbs into my throat. What if Dad isn't here? What if he is? My eyes are glued to the rows of houses.

1641. Four rusted numbers on an old metal mailbox—the sight almost takes my breath away. We're out of the car the instant it stops. We stand on the sidewalk, staring at the house. Mom takes our hands in hers, and together the three of us race up the walkway to the door of a brown one-story house with curtainless windows and beat-up siding. A trailer sits beside it.

Mom smiles down at us. Then she rings the bell.

"I'm comin', I'm comin'," says a voice from the other side of the door. A woman's voice.

Mom tightens her grip on my hand. The door flies open to reveal a pocket-sized woman wearing overalls and a headscarf.

"Yes?"

"I'm looking for someone. My *husband,*" Mom says. "Darryl Daniels? He wrote us a letter from this address."

The woman starts. "Yes, that's right. He did." She has a pair of glasses on a chain around her neck. She puts them on. "The big one looks just like him." The woman smiles at me, but it is a slow, sad smile and it doesn't stay put for long.

"Is he here?" Mom asks impatiently.

"No."

"No?"

The woman shifts nervously from foot to foot. "I'm sorry, miss. I rented my trailer out to him for a bit, a week, maybe a little more, but—"

"Do you mean that thing over there?"

Mom doesn't wait for an answer. She drops our hands

and runs at the trailer, a mountain of metal and grime, and bangs her fists on the door. "Darryl, you come out of there right now. I'm sick of this."

The trailer's windows are dark. No one answers Mom's cries. She pounds harder, the flimsy door shuddering with each blow of her fists, and screams, "You can't leave me like this!"

I run over to her, hollering "Mom, stop!" but Mom will not. She finds a new weapon—her feet—and kicks at the door again and again until I throw myself at her and wrap my arms around her waist.

"Mom, stop it!" I scream. "He's not here! Dad's not here!"

I feel Mom's chest heaving through her sweat-soaked T-shirt. I feel her body go rigid and then slack, and I know she's falling. I know it, but I don't let go. We land in a heap beside the trailer.

"He's not here," Mom says in a hollow voice.

"He's not?" I turn to find Tiffany standing behind me, tears running down her face. I let go of Mom, stand up, and reach for her. She pulls away.

"Liar!" Tiffany explodes at me. "You told me we'd find Dad and he'd take us to the perfect place. You're a liar!"

Tiffany crumples, joining Mom on the ground, the two of them broken. My face is wet with tears, though I can't remember when I started to cry. I hoped. I got the address. I promised Tiffany. And Dad is not here.

The woman comes over to us. "I'm sorry," she says. "I wish I knew where your daddy was headed, but he didn't say. He just left that letter to y'all and asked me to mail it off. When I saw that he hadn't put a return address on it, I did it for him and—I'm sorry. I didn't know y'all were looking for him. I didn't know he was running away."

Is it true what that lady said? I don't look at her, and I don't look at Mom and Tiffany, still on the ground. I can't. I take off running down the sidewalk instead.

Is Dad really running away? From us? I break into a sprint, trying to leave the questions behind me.

The breeze slips under my shorts and the sleeves of my T-shirt and it's like I'm flying. Is this what Dad feels when he moves from place to place? No wonder he can't stop. I can't either. Where will I go? As far away as I can get.

I hear something behind me. Voices. Calling my name. I run faster and then I fall, skinning my knee. I get up, run, and fall down again. When I try to get up this time, everything suddenly feels heavy, even the air around me. It's like someone's laid a stone on my chest. My breathing is loud and desperate. I reach into the pocket of my shorts for my inhaler, but it's too late. I know even before I take a puff. This asthma attack is too far gone. I yawn, and yawn again, as my brain tells my body to get more oxygen into my lungs.

That's when I hear footsteps slapping the pavement behind me. When the dark shapes around me start to get fuzzy and I begin to cough and can't stop, Mom throws herself down beside me. I hear her voice, frantic and far away, and feel her dry hands on my face.

"Wake up, Treasure. Open your eyes!"

I try. But I can't.

Thirty-Three

IN *and out. In and out.* Everything has been replaced by just one want: to breathe. *In and out. In and out.*

Am I going to die?

Thinking about it makes my breath catch in my throat. I cough and cough.

I concentrate on taking the deepest breaths I can, and on what I know. I know I am lying down in the back seat of Mom's truck. Tiffany is up front beside Mom, and the way my head keeps bouncing from side to side tells me Mom is not obeying the speed limit.

At last we come to a stop. Mom lifts me up and carries me, her arms shaking, into the too-bright light of the emergency room. I shut my eyes against it and am vaguely aware of the air whipping around me in a flurry of action. Questions are fired, Mom answers them, her voice still frantic. I feel myself being put down on a hard bed with cool sheets. I hear the quick metal-against-metal sound of a curtain being drawn. Soon someone lifts up my head and places a plastic mask over my mouth. I hear the flick of a switch and the gurgling sound of a nebulizer, releasing medicine into my lungs. In moments, my chest loosens and so does the rest of me. I'm okay now. The stone has been lifted from my chest. I'm not going to die. I open my eyes.

It's like a scene from a movie. The curtain is drawn and everyone is still. Mom sits in a folding chair, holding on to Tiffany, and the nurse is at the end of my bed, holding tight to a clipboard. When they notice that I'm awake . . . *Action!*

Mom and Tiffany come to the side of the bed. Tiffany pinches me—hard.

"You shouldn't have done that," she says firmly. I can see the dried tears on her face and the red around her nose and eyes. She climbs onto the narrow bed beside me and rests her head on my shoulder.

"I'm sorry," I say, my voice muffled by the mouthpiece.

The nurse consults her clipboard. "What triggered this attack?" she asks me.

"Running."

She looks puzzled. "Why?"

I shake my head. The nurse asks me about my inhaler and how often I use it. "The doctor will be in shortly," she says before disappearing through the curtain.

I look up at Mom. Her eyes are puffy and red. She reaches over and takes my hand. The doctor comes in then. He's young, white, and blonder than anyone I've ever seen.

He looks like he should be a plastic surgeon somewhere with white-sand beaches, not an emergency-room doctor down here in the sticks.

"Dr. Carr," he says, shaking Mom's free hand. "Treasure," he says, looking at my chart. "That's a fun name."

The nebulizer sputters, indicating the treatment is finished. Dr. Carr lifts the mask gently from my face and places it on the table next to me.

"I go by Jeanie."

"It's a shame to waste such a pretty name," he says, and smiles, flashing me two rows of perfect square teeth. "It seems that you've suffered what is known as an acute asthma attack."

Next to me, Tiffany sits up. "What do you mean, 'cute'? Her lips were blue!"

Now Dr. Carr blinds Tiffany with his smile. "A-cute. It means really, really bad. Now, it seems the breathing treatment was effective, but we're still going to send you home with five days' worth of oral medication. Steroids. Nurse Packer will give you the first dose here, and for the next four nights, you will take a decreasing dose at home, until all the medication is finished. Understood?"

At home? Where's that?

We all nod.

"Good." He folds up my paperwork. "You take care now, Treasure," the doctor says, and then he is gone.

I turn to Mom. "Did that lady say she knew where Dad went?" I ask.

"No. Your father has no intention of being found," Mom replies bitterly.

I wait for the weight of the truth to sink in: Dad really is running away from us. It stings, though not as much as I would've thought. Maybe I knew it all along. Maybe we all did.

"I almost forgot," Mom says, sitting up suddenly. "I bought this for you on the road." She reaches into the small leather backpack she sometimes uses as a purse and pulls out a pocket dictionary. She hands it to me. "It's not all fancy and leather-bound like your dad's, but—"

"I can carry words with me everywhere. It's perfect." I run my hands over the dictionary's cover. "So now what?" I ask.

Mom looks away. "Grace's," she says, and then quickly adds, "I'm sorry. We have nowhere else to go. I already called her."

I smile big, and so does Tiffany.

"Did I miss something?" Mom asks, just as the nurse returns with my medication and discharge papers. Mom helps me put my shorts and T-shirt back on, and then it's time for us to drive back to Auntie's. We've never gone back to a place before. I never knew it would feel so good.

Mom drives without the radio on, leaning against the door. I think about Dad's letter. *I'm sorry. I love you all.* My father knows tens of thousands of words, and for us he had only six.

"Where do you think he went?" Tiffany asks. She is stretched out in the back seat with Mr. Teddy Daniels.

"I don't know," Mom says in a flat voice. She lets the window down. A sweet, humid breeze sweeps through the car.

"Do you think we'll ever see him again?" Tiffany asks.

"Would we want to?" Mom replies.

Tiffany takes a long time to answer. "I don't know," she says at last, and she goes quiet after that.

I lean back in my seat, close my eyes, and picture it one last time. That perfect place I've been dreaming of since Dad left, the one he promised us he'd find. I see it like it's real, the sky-blue walls, sunlight pooled on the floors like melted butter, and the four of us together in it. I let the image dance before my eyes, and when the next breeze swoops through the car, I open my hands and let it go.

~~~~~

It's dark by the time Mom pulls onto Auntie's lawn. Auntie stands there, bathed in the glow of her porch light, and I wonder if she's been waiting in that spot since Mom called her from the hospital hours ago. She opens her front door and lets us in with all of our baggage. We collapse on her couch, worn out and, in my case, drugged up.

"I let y'all out of my sight for a minute and you're callin' me from the dang hospital." Auntie shakes her head.

She sits down in her brown armchair across from us. "I reckon now that you're back, we should get Miss Jaguar down to Goodies to start cleanin' shelves. What do you say to tomorrow?"

"Who's Miss Jaguar?" Mom asks.

We fill her all the way in, and by the time we come to the end of the story and Auntie's blank security tape, Mom is laughing so hard she's crying. I try to remember the last time she really laughed—the last time she threw her head back and opened her mouth so wide I could see her silver fillings—but I can't. Her laugh isn't pretty. It's half hiccup, half cackle, and it's the most beautiful sound I've ever heard.

We sit together in Auntie's living room until well after midnight, talking and laughing until Mom says, "I guess we'll stay here for a bit. Do you mind the extra company, Grace?"

"Not at all, but you'll be bunkin' in here with Mr. Shuffle, and y'all better follow my rules."

Tiffany and I groan.

"And you'll be needin' a job, Miss Lisa," Auntie says. Mom nods. "You can work in my store. Lord knows I'm gettin' too old to run that place by myself."

"Ohhhh. Okay," Mom says slowly.

"You can't handle the register," Tiffany tells her. "That's my job."

"You can supervise Jaguar with Treasure," Auntie says. "I reckon that'll be a hoot and a half."

I open my mouth to remind her that I'm going by Jeanie now, but I snap it shut. Maybe it's not so bad to go by Treasure again. Nestled on the couch between Mom and Tiffany, I look around Auntie's living room, with its clutter and junk and old, grimy figurines. Mr. Shuffle waddles in and joins Auntie in the armchair.

This is nothing like the perfect place I imagined we'd live in with Dad. Not at all. Auntie catches my eye and smiles.

It's better.